Selected Stories by
MARK TWAIN

Books in this Series:

Selected Stories by
MARK TWAIN

RUPA

Published by
Rupa Publications India Pvt. Ltd. 2014
161-B/4, Gulmohar House,
Yusuf Sarai Community Centre,
New Delhi 110049

Sales centres:

Bengaluru Chennai
Hyderabad Kolkata Mumbai

P-ISBN: 978-81-291-3141-6
E-ISBN: 978-81-291-4244-3

Sixth impression 2025

10 9 8 7 6

Printed in India

CONTENTS

INTRODUCTION

Samuel Langhorne Clemens (30 November 1835—21 April 1910), better known by his pen name Mark Twain, was an American author and humorist. Over the years, journalists and scholars have offered competing theories as to where America's first signature wit acquired his nom de plume. According to Twain, his pen name once belonged to a Mississippi riverboat captain, and he merely 'laid violent hands upon it.'

- 'The Story of the Bad Little Boy' is the story of a young boy who acts like the bad boys who are in the Sunday school books but things do not go horribly wrong for him...
- 'The Story of the Good Little Boy' is the story of a young boy who does everything right, never lies, never cheats, never steals and yet bad things happen to him.
- 'Journalism in Tennessee' is about how Tennessee journalism is biased, is the story of how based on the whims of the swashbuckling, violent populace instead of a disinterested quest for the truth.
- In 'A Curious Dream' the narrator describes and comments upon a singular dream he had.
- 'How I Edited an Agricultural Paper' is the story of what happens when Mark Twain takes over an agriculture magazine.
- In 'The £1,000,000 Bank-Note' two very rich, eccentric brothers give the penniless protagonist Henry Adams one million pounds in the form of a single peerless bank note.

- 'The Invalid's Story' is the story of what happens when a man goes on a train to take his friend's corpse to his parents house.
- 'A Telephonic Conversation' recounts an overheard conversation in a home at a time when the majority of Americans had never yet heard a voice via a telephone.
- 'Italian with Grammar' tells the story of what happens when the verb is the centre of a storm.
- 'The Private History of a Campaign That Failed' is about a group of inexperienced militiamen, who kill an innocent horseman mistaking him for a Yankee scout.
- In 'Luck' a total idiot triumphs in life through sheer good luck.
- 'Italian Without A Master' is about the narrator's adventures in learning Italian.
- 'A Burlesque Biography' is about what happens when one writes an autobiography and yields at last to frenzied public demand.
- In 'The Celebrated Jumping Frog of Calaveras County' the narrator retells a story he heard from a bartender, Simon Wheeler.
- 'Was It Heaven? Or Hell?' is a story that dissects the conventional wisdom of truth-telling—from verbal to non-verbal lying.

THE STORY OF THE BAD LITTLE BOY

Once this little bad boy stole the key of the pantry, and slipped in there and helped himself to some jam, and filled up the vessel with tar so that his mother would never know the difference; but all at once a terrible feeling didn't come over him, and something didn't seem to whisper to him, 'Is it right to disobey my mother? Isn't it sinful to do this? Where do bad little boys go who gobble up their good kind mother's jam?' and then he didn't kneel down all alone and promise never to be wicked any more, and rise up with a light, happy heart, and go and tell his mother all about it and beg her forgiveness, and be blessed by her with tears of pride and thankfulness in her eyes. No; that is the way with all other bad boys in the books; but it happened otherwise with this Jim, strangely enough. He ate that jam, and said it was bully, in his sinful, vulgar way; and he put in the tar, and said that was bully also, and laughed, and observed 'that the old woman would get up and snort' when she found it out; and when she did find it out, he denied knowing anything about it, and she whipped him severely, and he did the crying himself. Everything about this boy was curious—everything turned out differently with him from the way it does to the bad Jameses in the books.

Once he climbed up in Farmer Acorn's apple tree to steal apples, and the limb didn't break, and he didn't fall and break his arm, and get torn by the farmer's great dog, and then languish on a sick bed for weeks, and repent and become good. Oh! no; he stole as many apples as he wanted and came down all right; and he was all ready for the dog too, and knocked him endways with a brick when he came to tear him. It was very strange—nothing like it ever happened in those mild little books with marbled backs, and with pictures in them of men with swallow-tailed coats and bell-crowned hats, and pantaloons that are short in the legs, and women with the waists of their dresses under their arms, and no hoops on. Nothing like it in any of the Sunday-school books.

Once he stole the teacher's penknife, and, when he was afraid it would be found out and he would get whipped, he slipped it into George Wilson's cap—poor Widow Wilson's son, the moral boy, the good little boy of the village, who always obeyed his mother, and never told an untruth, and was fond of his lessons, and infatuated with Sunday school. And when the knife dropped from the cap, and poor George hung his head and blushed, as if in conscious guilt, and the grieved teacher charged the theft upon him, and was just in the very act of bringing the switch down upon his trembling shoulders, a white-haired, improbable justice of the peace did not suddenly appear in their midst, and strike an attitude and say, 'Spare this noble boy—there stands the cowering culprit! I was passing the school door at recess, and unseen myself, I saw the theft committed!' And then Jim didn't get whaled, and the venerable justice didn't read the tearful school a homily, and take George by the hand and say such a boy deserved to be exalted, and then tell him to come and make his home with him, and sweep out the office, and make fires, and run errands, and chop wood, and study law, and help his wife do household labors, and have all the balance of the time to play, and get forty cents a month, and be happy. No; it would have happened that way in the books, but it didn't happen that way to Jim. No meddling old clam of a justice dropped in to make trouble, and so the model boy

George got thrashed, and Jim was glad of it. Because, you know, Jim hated moral boys. Jim said he was 'down on them milksops.' Such was the coarse language of this bad, neglected boy.

But the strangest thing that ever happened to Jim was the time he went boating on Sunday, and didn't get drowned, and that other time that he got caught out in the storm when he was fishing on Sunday, and didn't get struck by lightning. Why, you might look, and look, and look, all through the Sunday school books from now till next Christmas, and you would never come across anything like this. Oh no; you would find that all the bad boys who go boating on Sunday invariably get drowned, and all the bad boys who get caught out in storms, when they are fishing on Sunday, infallibly get struck by lightning. Boats with bad boys in them are always upset on Sunday, and it always storms when bad boys go fishing on the Sabbath. How this Jim ever escaped is a mystery to me.

And he grew up, and married, and raised a large family, and brained them all with an axe one night, and got wealthy by all manner of cheating and rascality; and now he is the infernalest wickedest scoundrel in his native village, and is universally respected, and belongs to the Legislature.

So you see there never was a bad James in the Sunday school books that had such a streak of luck as this sinful Jim with the charmed life.

2

THE STORY OF
THE GOOD LITTLE BOY

This good little boy read all the Sunday school books; they were his greatest delight. This was the whole secret of it. He believed in the good little boys they put in the Sunday school books; he had every confidence in them. He longed to come across one of them alive, once; but he never did. They all died before his time, maybe. Whenever he read about a particularly good one, he turned over quickly to the end to see what became of him, because he wanted to travel thousands of miles and gaze on him; but it wasn't any use; that good little boy always died in the last chapter, and there was a picture of the funeral, with all his relations and the Sunday school children standing around the grave in pantaloons that were too short, and bonnets that were too large, and everybody crying into handkerchiefs that had as much as a yard and a half of stuff in them. He was always headed off in this way. He never could see one of those good little boys on account of his always dying in the last chapter.

Jacob had a noble ambition to be put in a Sunday school book. He wanted to be put in, with pictures representing him gloriously declining to lie to his mother, and her weeping for joy about it; and pictures representing him standing on the doorstep giving a penny to a poor beggar-woman with six children, and telling her to spend it freely, but not to be extravagant, because extravagance is a sin; and pictures of him magnanimously refusing to tell on the bad boy who always lay in wait for him around the corner as he came from school, and welted him over the head with a lath, and then chased him home, saying, 'Hi! hi!' as he proceeded. That was the ambition of young Jacob Blivens. He wished to be put in a Sunday school book. It made him feel a little uncomfortable sometimes when he reflected that the good little boys always died. He loved to live, you know, and this was the most unpleasant feature about being a Sunday-schoolbook boy. He knew it was not healthy to be good. He knew it was more fatal than consumption to be so supernaturally good as the boys in the books were; he knew that none of them had ever been able to stand it long, and it pained him to think that if they put him in a book he wouldn't ever see it, or even if they did get the book out before he died it wouldn't be popular without any picture of his funeral in the back part of it. It couldn't be much of a Sunday-school book that couldn't tell about the advice he gave to the community when he was dying. So at last, of course he had to make up his mind to do the best he could under the circumstances—to live right, and hang on as long as he could, and have his dying speech ready when his time came.

But somehow, nothing ever went right with this good little boy; nothing ever turned out with him the way it turned out with boys in the books. They always had a good time, and the bad boys had the broken legs; but in his case there was a screw loose somewhere, and it all happened just the other way. When he found Jim Blake stealing apples, and went under the tree to read to him about the bad little boy who fell out of a neighbor's apple-tree and broke his arm, Jim fell out of the tree too, but he fell on him, and broke his arm, and Jim wasn't hurt at all. Jacob couldn't understand that. There wasn't anything in the books like it.

And once, when some bad boys pushed a blind man over in

the mud, and Jacob ran to help him up and receive his blessing, the blind man did not give him any blessing at all, but whacked him over the head with his stick and said he would like to catch him shoving him again, and then pretending to help him up. This was not in accordance with any of the books. Jacob looked them all over to see.

One thing that Jacob wanted to do was to find a lame dog that hadn't any place to stay, and was hungry and persecuted, and bring him home and pet him and have that dog's imperishable gratitude. And at last, he found one and was happy; and he brought him home and fed him, but when he was going to pet him the dog flew at him and tore all the clothes off him except those that were in front, and made a spectacle of him that was astonishing. He examined authorities, but he could not understand the matter. It was of the same breed of dogs that was in the books, but it acted very differently. Whatever this boy did, he got into trouble. The very things the boys in the books got rewarded for, turned out to be about the most unprofitable things he could invest in.

Once, when he was on his way to Sunday-school, he saw some bad boys starting off pleasuring in a sail-boat. He was filled with consternation, because he knew from his reading that boys who went sailing on Sunday invariably got drowned. So he ran out on a raft to warn them, but a log turned with him and slid him into the river. A man got him out pretty soon, and the doctor pumped the water out of him, and gave him a fresh start with his bellows, but he caught cold and lay sick in bed nine weeks. But the most unaccountable thing about it was that the bad boys in the boat had a good time all day, and then reached home alive and well in the most surprising manner. Jacob Blivens said there was nothing like these things in the books. He was perfectly dumbfounded.

When he got well he was a little discouraged, but he resolved to keep on trying anyhow. He knew that so far his experiences wouldn't do to go in a book, but he hadn't yet reached the allotted term of life for good little boys, and he hoped to be able to make a record yet, if he could hold on till his time was fully up. If everything else failed, he had his dying speech to fall back on.

He examined his authorities, and found that it was now time for him to go to sea as a cabin-boy. He called on a ship captain and made his application, and when the captain asked for his recommendations he proudly drew out a tract and pointed to the words, 'To Jacob Blivens, from his affectionate teacher.' But the captain was a coarse, vulgar man, and he said, 'Oh, that be blowed! that wasn't any proof that he knew how to wash dishes or handle a slush-bucket, and he guessed he didn't want him.' This was altogether the most extraordinary thing that ever happened to Jacob in all his life. A compliment from a teacher, on a tract, had never failed to move the tenderest emotions of ship captains, and open the way to all offices of honor and profit in their gift— it never had in any book that ever he had read. He could hardly believe his senses.

This boy always had a hard time of it. Nothing ever came out according to the authorities with him. At last, one day, when he was around hunting up bad little boys to admonish, he found a lot of them in an old iron foundry fixing up a little joke on fourteen or fifteen dogs, which they had tied together in long procession and were going to ornament with empty nitroglycerine cans made fast to their tails. Jacob's heart was touched. He sat down on one of those cans—for he never minded grease when duty was before him—and he took hold of the foremost dog by the collar, and turned his reproving eye upon wicked Tom Jones. But just at that moment, Alderman McWelter, full of wrath, stepped in. All the bad boys ran away, but Jacob Blivens rose in conscious innocence and began one of those stately little Sunday-school book speeches which always commence with 'Oh, sir!' in dead opposition to the fact that no boy, good or bad, ever starts a remark with 'Oh, sir!' But the Alderman never waited to hear the rest. He took Jacob

Blivens by the ear and turned him around, and hit him a whack in the rear with the flat of his hand; and in an instant that good little boy shot out through the roof and soared away towards the sun, with the fragments of those fifteen dogs stringing after him like the tail of a kite. And there wasn't a sign of that Alderman or that old iron foundry left on the face of the earth, and, as for young Jacob Blivens, he never got a chance to make his last dying speech after all his trouble fixing it up, unless he made it to the birds; because, although the bulk of him came down all right in a tree-top in an adjoining county, the rest of him was apportioned around among four townships, and so they had to hold five inquests on him to find out whether he was dead or not, and how it occurred. You never saw a boy scattered so.

Thus perished the good little boy who did the best he could, but didn't come out according to the books. Every boy who ever did as he did prospered except him. His case is truly remarkable. It will probably never be accounted for.

3

JOURNALISM IN TENNESSEE

The editor of the Memphis Avalanche swoops thus mildly down upon a correspondent who posted him as a Radical: 'While he was writing the first word, the middle, dotting his i's, crossing his t's, and punching his period, he knew he was concocting a sentence that was saturated with infamy and reeking with falsehood.'—Exchange.

I was told by the physician that a Southern climate would improve my health, and so I went down to Tennessee, and got a berth on the Morning Glory and Johnson County War—Whoop as associate editor. When I went on duty, I found the chief editor sitting tilted back in a three-legged chair with his feet on a pine table. There was another pine table in the room and another afflicted chair, and both were half buried under newspapers and scraps and sheets of manuscript. There was a wooden box of sand, sprinkled with cigar stubs and 'old soldiers,' and a stove with a door hanging by its upper hinge. The chief editor had a long-tailed black cloth frock-coat on, and white linen pants. His boots were small and neatly blacked. He wore a ruffled shirt, a large seal-ring, a standing collar of obsolete pattern, and a checkered neckerchief with the ends hanging down. Date of costume about 1848. He was smoking a cigar, and trying to think of a word, and in pawing his hair he had rumpled his locks a good deal. He was scowling fearfully, and I judged that he was concocting a particularly knotty editorial. He told me to take the exchanges and skim through them and write up the 'Spirit of the Tennessee Press,' condensing into the article, all of their contents that seemed of interest.

I wrote as follows:

SPIRIT OF THE TENNESSEE PRESS

The editors of the Semi-Weekly Earthquake evidently labor under a misapprehension with regard to the Dallyhack railroad. It is not the object of the company to leave Buzzardville off to one side. On the contrary, they consider it one of the most important points along the line, and consequently can have no desire to slight it. The gentlemen of the Earthquake will, of course, take pleasure in making the correction.

John W. Blossom, Esq., the able editor of the Higginsville Thunderbolt and Battle Cry of Freedom, arrived in the city yesterday. He is stopping at the Van Buren House.

We observe that our contemporary of the Mud Springs Morning Howl has fallen into the error of supposing that the election of Van Werter is not an established fact, but he will have discovered his mistake before this reminder reaches him, no doubt. He was doubtless misled by incomplete election returns.

It is pleasant to note that the city of Blathersville is endeavoring to contract with some New York gentlemen to pave its well-nigh impassable streets with the Nicholson pavement. The Daily Hurrah urges the measure with ability, and seems confident of ultimate success.

I passed my manuscript over to the chief editor for acceptance, alteration, or destruction. He glanced at it and his face clouded. He ran his eye down the pages, and his countenance grew portentous. It was easy to see that something was wrong. Presently, he sprang up and said:

'Thunder and lightning! Do you suppose I am going to speak of those cattle that way? Do you suppose my subscribers are going to stand such gruel as that? Give me the pen!'

I never saw a pen scrape and scratch its way so viciously, or plow through another man's verbs and adjectives so relentlessly. While he was in the midst of his work, somebody shot at him through the open window, and marred the symmetry of my ear.

'Ah,' said he, 'that is that scoundrel Smith, of the Moral Volcano—he was due yesterday.' And he snatched a navy revolver from his belt and fired—Smith dropped, shot in the thigh. The shot spoiled Smith's aim, who was just taking a second chance and he crippled a stranger. It was me. Merely a finger shot off.

Then the chief editor went on with his erasure; and interlineations. Just as he finished them, a hand grenade came down the stove-pipe, and the explosion shivered the stove into a thousand fragments. However, it did no further damage, except that a vagrant piece knocked a couple of my teeth out.

'That stove is utterly ruined,' said the chief editor.

I said I believed it was.

'Well, no matter—don't want it this kind of weather. I know the man that did it. I'll get him. Now, here is the way this stuff ought to be written.'

I took the manuscript. It was scarred with erasures and interlineations till its mother wouldn't have known it, if it had had one. It now read as follows:

SPIRIT OF THE TENNESSEE PRESS

The inveterate liars of the Semi-Weekly Earthquake are evidently endeavoring to palm off upon a noble and chivalrous people another of their vile and brutal falsehoods with regard to that most glorious conception of the nineteenth century, the Ballyhack railroad. The idea that Buzzardville was to be left off at one side originated in their own fulsome brains—or rather in the settlings which they regard as brains. They had better, swallow this lie if they want to save their abandoned reptile carcasses the cowhiding they so richly deserve.

That ass, Blossom, of the Higginsville Thunderbolt and Battle Cry of Freedom, is down here again sponging at the Van Buren.

We observe that the besotted blackguard of the Mud Springs Morning Howl is giving out, with his usual propensity for lying, that Van Werter is not elected. The heaven-born mission of journalism is to disseminate truth; to eradicate error; to educate, refine, and elevate the tone of public morals and manners, and make all men more gentle, more virtuous, more charitable, and in all ways better, and holier, and happier; and yet this blackhearted scoundrel degrades his great office persistently to the dissemination of falsehood, calumny, vituperation, and vulgarity.

Blathersville wants a Nicholson pavement—it wants a jail and a poorhouse more. The idea of a pavement in a one-horse town composed of two gin-mills, a blacksmith shop, and that mustard-plaster of a newspaper, *The Daily Hurrah!* The crawling insect, Buckner, who edits *The Hurrah*, is braying about his business with his customary imbecility, and imagining that he is talking sense.

'Now that is the way to write—peppery and to the point. Mush-and-milk journalism gives me the fan-tods.'

About this time a brick came through the window with a splintering crash, and gave me a considerable of a jolt in the back. I moved out of range—I began to feel in the way.

The chief said, 'That was the Colonel, likely. I've been expecting him for two days. He will be up now right away.'

He was correct. The Colonel appeared in the door a moment afterward with a dragoon revolver in his hand.

He said, 'Sir, have I the honor of addressing the poltroon who edits this mangy sheet?'

'You have. Be seated, sir. Be careful of the chair, one of its legs is gone. I believe I have the honor of addressing the putrid liar, Colonel Blatherskite Tecumseh?'

'Right, Sir. I have a little account to settle with you. If you are at leisure we will begin.'

'I have an article on the 'Encouraging Progress of Moral and Intellectual Development in America' to finish, but there is no hurry. Begin.'

Both pistols rang out their fierce clamor at the same instant. The chief lost a lock of his hair, and the Colonel's bullet ended its career in the fleshy part of my thigh. The Colonel's left shoulder was clipped a little. They fired again. Both missed their men this time, but I got my share, a shot in the arm. At the third fire both gentlemen were wounded slightly, and I had a knuckle chipped. I then said, I believed I would go out and take a walk, as this was a private matter, and I had a delicacy about participating in it further. But both gentlemen begged me to keep my seat, and assured me that I was not in the way.

They then talked about the elections and the crops while they reloaded, and I fell to tying up my wounds. But presently, they opened fire again with animation, and every shot took effect—but it is proper to remark that five out of the six fell to my share. The sixth one mortally wounded the Colonel, who remarked, with fine humor, that he would have to say good morning now, as he had business uptown. He then inquired the way to the undertaker's and left.

The chief turned to me and said, 'I am expecting company to dinner, and shall have to get ready. It will be a favor to me if you will read proof and attend to the customers.'

I winced a little at the idea of attending to the customers, but I was too bewildered by the fusillade that was still ringing in my ears to think of anything to say.

He continued, 'Jones will be here at three—cowhide him. Gillespie will call earlier, perhaps—throw him out of the window. Ferguson will be along about four—kill him. That is all for today, I believe. If you have any odd time, you may write a blistering article on the police—give the chief inspector rats. The cowhides are under the table; weapons in the drawer—ammunition there in the corner—lint and bandages up there in the pigeonholes. In case of accident, go to Lancet, the surgeon, down- stairs. He advertises—we take it out in trade.'

He was gone. I shuddered. At the end of the next three hours, I had been through perils so awful that all peace of mind and all cheerfulness were gone from me. Gillespie had called and thrown me out of the window. Jones arrived promptly, and when I got ready to do the cowhiding, he took the job off my hands. In an encounter with a stranger, not in the bill of fare, I had lost my scalp. Another stranger, by the name of Thompson, left me a mere wreck and ruin of chaotic rags. And at last, at bay in the corner, and beset by an infuriated mob of editors, blacklegs, politicians, and desperadoes, who raved and swore and flourished their weapons about my head till the air shimmered with glancing flashes of steel, I was in the act of resigning my berth on the paper when the chief arrived, and with him a rabble of charmed and enthusiastic friends. Then ensued a scene of riot and carnage such as no human pen, or steel one either, could describe. People were shot, probed, dismembered, blown up, thrown out of the window. There was a brief tornado of murky blasphemy, with a confused and frantic war-dance glimmering through it, and then all was over. In five minutes there was silence, and the gory chief and I sat alone and surveyed the sanguinary ruin that strewed the floor around us.

He said, 'You'll like this place when you get used to it.'

I said, 'I'll have to get you to excuse me; I think maybe I might write to suit you after a while; as soon as I had had some practice and learned the language I am confident I could. But, to speak the plain truth, that sort of energy of expression has its inconveniences, and a, man is liable to interruption.

'You see that yourself. Vigorous writing is calculated to elevate the public, no doubt, but then I do not like to attract so much attention as it calls forth. I can't write with comfort when I am interrupted so much as I have been today. I like this berth well enough, but I don't like to be left here to wait on the customers. The experiences are novel, I grant you, and entertaining, too, after a fashion, but they are not judiciously distributed. A gentleman shoots at you through the window and cripples me; a bombshell comes down the stovepipe for your gratification and sends the stove door down my throat; a friend drops in to swap compliments with you, and freckles me with bullet-holes till my skin won't hold my principles; you go to dinner, and Jones comes with his cowhide, Gillespie throws me out of the window, Thompson tears all my clothes off, and an entire stranger takes my scalp with the easy freedom of an old acquaintance; and in less than five minutes all the blackguards in the country arrive in their war-paint, and proceed to scare the rest of me to death with their tomahawks. Take it altogether, I never had such a spirited time in all my life as I have had today. No; I like you, and I like your calm unruffled way of explaining things to the customers, but you see I am not used to it. The Southern heart is too impulsive; Southern hospitality is too lavish with the stranger. The paragraphs which I have written today, and into whose cold sentences your masterly hand has infused the fervent spirit of Tennesseean journalism, will wake up another nest of hornets. All that mob of editors will come—and they will come hungry, too, and want somebody for breakfast. I shall have to bid you adieu. I decline to be present at these festivities. I came South for my health, I will go back on the same errand, and suddenly. Tennesseean journalism is too stirring for me.'

After which we parted with mutual regret, and I took apartments at the hospital.

4

A CURIOUS DREAM

Night before last, I had a singular dream. I seemed to be sitting on a doorstep (in no particular city perhaps) ruminating, and the time of night appeared to be about twelve or one o'clock. The weather was balmy and delicious. There was no human sound in the air, not even a footstep. There was no sound of any kind to emphasize the dead stillness, except the occasional hollow barking of a dog in the distance and the fainter answer of a further dog. Presently up the street, I heard a bony clack-clacking, and guessed it was the castanets of a serenading party. In a minute more, a tall skeleton, hooded, and half clad in a tattered and moldy shroud, whose shreds were flapping about the ribby latticework of its person, swung by me with a stately stride and disappeared in the gray gloom of the starlight. It had a broken and worm-eaten coffin on its shoulder and a bundle of something in its hand. I knew what the clack-clacking was then; it was this party's joints working together, and his elbows knocking against his sides as he walked. I may say, I was surprised. Before I could collect my thoughts and enter upon any speculations as to what this apparition might portend, I heard another one coming for I recognized his clack-clack. He had two-thirds of a coffin on his shoulder, and some foot and head boards under his arm. I mightily wanted, to peer under his hood and speak to him, but when he turned and smiled upon me with his cavernous sockets and his projecting grin as he went by, I thought I would not detain him. He was hardly gone when I heard the clacking again, and another one issued from the shadowy half-light. This one was bending under a heavy gravestone, and dragging a shabby coffin after him by a string. When he got to me he gave me a steady look for a moment or two, and then rounded to and backed up to me, saying: 'Ease this down for a fellow, will you?'

I eased the gravestone down till it rested on the ground, and in doing so noticed that it bore the name of 'John Baxter Copmanhurst,' with 'May, 1839,' as the date of his death. Deceased sat wearily down by me, and wiped his os frontis with his major maxillary—chiefly from former habit I judged, for I could not see that he brought away any perspiration.

'It is too bad, too bad,' said he, drawing the remnant of the shroud about him and leaning his jaw pensively on his hand. Then he put his left foot up on his knee and fell to scratching his anklebone absently with a rusty nail which he got out of his coffin.

'What is too bad, friend?'

'Oh, everything, everything. I almost wish I never had died.'

'You surprise me. Why do you say this? Has anything gone wrong? What is the matter?'

'Matter! Look at this shroud-rags. Look at this gravestone, all battered up. Look at that disgraceful old coffin. All a man's property going to ruin and destruction before his eyes, and ask him if anything is wrong? Fire and brimstone!'

'Calm yourself, calm yourself,' I said. 'It is too bad-it is certainly too bad, but then I had not supposed that you would much mind such matters situated as you are.'

'Well, my dear sir, I do mind them. My pride is hurt, and my comfort is impaired—destroyed, I might say. I will state my case—I will put it to you in such a way that you can comprehend it, if you will let me,' said the poor skeleton, tilting the hood of his shroud back, as if he were clearing for action, and thus unconsciously giving himself a jaunty and festive air very much at variance with the grave character of his position in life—so to speak—and in prominent contrast with his distressful mood.

'Proceed,' said I.

'I reside in the shameful old graveyard a block or two above you here, in this street—there, now, I just expected that cartilage would let go!—third rib from the bottom, friend, hitch the end of it to my spine with a string, if you have got such a thing about you, though a bit of silver wire is a deal pleasanter, and more durable and becoming, if one keeps it polished—to think of shredding out and going to pieces in this way, just on account of the indifference and neglect of one's posterity!'—and the poor ghost grated his teeth in a way that gave me a wrench and a shiver—for the effect is mightily increased by the absence of muffling flesh and cuticle. 'I reside in that old graveyard, and have for these thirty years; and I tell you things are changed since I first laid this old tired frame there, and turned over, and stretched out for a long sleep, with a delicious sense upon me of being done with bother, and grief, and anxiety, and doubt, and fear, forever and ever, and listening with comfortable and increasing satisfaction to the sexton's work, from the startling clatter of his first spadeful on my coffin till it dulled away to the faint patting that shaped the roof of my new home-delicious! My! I wish you could try it tonight!' and out of my reverie deceased fetched me a rattling slap with a bony hand.

'Yes, sir, thirty years ago I laid me down there, and was happy. For it was out in the country then—out in the breezy, flowery, grand old woods, and the lazy winds gossiped with the leaves, and the squirrels capered over us and around us, and the creeping things visited us, and the birds filled the tranquil solitude with music. Ah, it was worth ten years of a man's life to be dead then! Everything was pleasant. I was in a good neighborhood, for all the dead people that lived near me belonged to the best families in the city. Our posterity appeared to think the world of us. They kept our graves in the very best condition; the fences were always in faultless repair, head-boards were kept painted or whitewashed, and were replaced with new ones as soon as they began to look rusty or decayed; monuments were kept upright, railings intact and bright, the rose-bushes and shrubbery trimmed, trained, and free from blemish, the walks clean and smooth and graveled. But that day is gone by. Our descendants have forgotten us. My grandson lives in a stately house built with money made by these old hands of mine, and I sleep in a neglected grave with invading vermin that gnaw my shroud to build them nests withal! I and friends that lie with me founded and secured the prosperity of this fine city, and the stately bantling of our loves leaves us to rot in a dilapidated cemetery which neighbors curse and strangers scoff at. See the difference between the old time and this —for instance: Our graves are all caved in now; our head-boards have rotted away and tumbled down; our railings reel this way and that, with one foot in the air, after a fashion of unseemly levity; our monuments lean wearily, and our gravestones bow their heads discouraged; there be no adornments any more—no roses, nor shrubs, nor graveled walks, nor anything that is a comfort to the eye; and even the paintless old board fence that did make a show of holding us sacred from companionship with beasts and the defilement of heedless feet, has tottered till it overhangs the street, and only advertises the presence of our dismal resting-place and invites yet more derision to it. And now we cannot hide our poverty and tatters in the friendly woods, for the city has stretched its withering arms abroad and taken us in, and all that remains of the cheer of our old home is the cluster of lugubrious forest trees that stand, bored and weary of a city life, with their feet in our coffins, looking into the hazy distance and wishing they were there. I tell you it is disgraceful!

'You begin to comprehend—you begin to see how it is. While

our descendants are living sumptuously on our money, right around us in the city, we have to fight hard to keep skull and bones together. Bless you, there isn't a grave in our cemetery that doesn't leak not one. Every time it rains in the night, we have to climb out and roost in the trees and sometimes we are wakened suddenly by the chilly water trickling down the back of our necks. Then I tell you there is a general heaving up of old graves and kicking over of old monuments, and scampering of old skeletons for the trees! Bless me, if you had gone along there some such nights after twelve, you might have seen as many as fifteen of us roosting on one limb, with our joints rattling drearily and the wind wheezing through our ribs! Many a time we have perched there for three or four dreary hours, and then come down, stiff and chilled through and drowsy, and borrowed each other's skulls to bail out our graves with—if you will glance up in my mouth now as I tilt my head back, you can see that my head-piece is half full of old dry sediment how top-heavy and stupid it makes me sometimes! Yes, sir, many a time if you had happened to come along just before the dawn you'd have caught us bailing out the graves and hanging our shrouds on the fence to dry. Why, I had an elegant shroud stolen from there one morning—think a party by the name of Smith took it, that resides in a plebeian graveyard over yonder—I think so because the first time I ever saw him he hadn't anything on but a check shirt, and the last time I saw him, which was at a social gathering in the new cemetery, he was the best-dressed corpse in the company—and it is a significant fact that he left when he saw me; and presently an old woman from here missed her coffin—she generally took it with her when she went anywhere, because she was liable to take cold and bring on the spasmodic rheumatism that originally killed her if she exposed herself to the night air much. She was named Hotchkiss—Anna Matilda Hotchkiss—you might know her? She has two upper front teeth, is tall, but a good deal inclined to stoop, one rib on the left side gone, has one shred of rusty hair hanging from the left side of her head, and one little tuft just above and a little forward of her right ear, has her underjaw wired on one side where it had worked loose, small bone of left forearm gone—lost in a fight has a kind of swagger in her gait and a 'gallus' way of going with: her arms akimbo and her nostrils in the air has been pretty free and easy, and is all damaged and battered up till she looks like a queensware crate in ruins—maybe you have met her?'

'God forbid!' I involuntarily ejaculated, for somehow I was not looking for that form of question, and it caught me a little off my guard. But I hastened to make amends for my rudeness, and say, 'I simply meant I had not had the honor—for I would not deliberately speak discourteously of a friend of yours. You were saying that you were robbed—and it was a shame, too—but it appears by what is left of the shroud you have on that it was a costly one in its day. How did—'

A most ghastly expression began to develop among the decayed features and shriveled integuments of my guest's face, and I was beginning to grow uneasy and distressed, when he told me he was only working up a deep, sly smile, with a wink in it, to suggest that about the time he acquired his present garment a ghost in a neighboring cemetery missed one. This reassured me, but I begged him to confine himself to speech thenceforth, because his facial expression was uncertain. Even with the most elaborate care it was liable to miss fire. Smiling should especially be avoided. What he might honestly consider a shining success was likely to strike me in a very different light. I said I liked to see a skeleton cheerful, even decorously playful, but I did not think smiling was a skeleton's best hold.

'Yes, friend,' said the poor skeleton, 'the facts are just as I have given them to you. Two of these old graveyards—the one that I resided in and one further along have been deliberately neglected by our descendants of today, until there is no occupying them any longer. Aside from the osteological discomfort of it—and that is no light matter this rainy weather—the present state of things is ruinous to property. We have got to move or be content to see our effects wasted away and utterly destroyed.

'Now, you will hardly believe it, but it is true, nevertheless, that there isn't a single coffin in good repair among all my acquaintance—now that is an absolute fact. I do not refer to low people who come in a pine box mounted on an express-wagon, but I am talking about your high-toned, silver-mounted burial-case, your monumental sort, that travel under black plumes at the head of a procession and have choice of cemetery lots— I mean folks like the Jarvises, and the Bledsoes and Burlings, and such. They are all about ruined. The most substantial people in our set, they were. And now look at them—utterly used up and poverty-stricken. One of the Bledsoes actually traded his monument to a late barkeeper for some fresh shavings to put under his head. I tell you it speaks volumes, for there is nothing a corpse takes so much pride in as his monument. He loves to read the inscription. He comes after a while to believe what it says himself, and then you may see him sitting on the fence night after night enjoying it. Epitaphs are cheap, and they do a poor chap a world of good after he is dead, especially if he had hard luck while he was alive. I wish they were used more. Now I don't complain, but confidentially I do think it was a little shabby in my descendants to give me nothing but this old slab of a gravestone—and all the more that there isn't a compliment on it. It used to have "GONE TO HIS JUST REWARD" on it, and I was proud when I first saw it, but by and by I noticed that whenever an old friend of mine came along he would hook his chin on the railing and pull a long face and read along down till he came to that, and then he would chuckle to himself and walk off, looking satisfied and comfortable. So I scratched it off to get rid of those fools. But a dead man always takes a deal of pride in his monument. Yonder goes half a dozen of the Jarvises now, with the family monument along. And Smithers and some hired specters went by with his awhile ago. Hello, Higgins, good-bye, old friend! That's Meredith Higgins—died in '44— belongs to our set in the cemetery—fine old family—great-grand mother was an Injun—I am on the most familiar terms with him, he didn't hear me was the reason he didn't answer me. And I am sorry, too, because I would have liked to introduce you. You would admire him. He is the most disjointed, sway-backed, and generally distorted old skeleton you ever saw, but he is full of fun. When he laughs it sounds like rasping two stones together, and he always starts it off with a cheery screech like raking a nail across a window-pane. Hey, Jones! That is old Columbus Jones—shroud cost four hundred dollars entire trousseau, including monument, twenty-seven hundred. This was in the spring of '26. It was enormous style for those days. Dead people came all the way from the Alleghanies to see his things—the party that occupied the grave next to mine remembers it well. Now do you see that individual going along with a piece of a head-board under his arm, one leg-bone below his knee gone, and not a thing in the world on? That is Barstow Dalhousie, and next to Columbus Jones he was the most sumptuously outfitted person that ever entered our cemetery. We are all leaving. We cannot tolerate the treatment we are receiving at the hands of our descendants. They open new cemeteries, but they leave us to our ignominy. They mend the streets, but they never mend anything that is about us or belongs to us. Look at that coffin of mine—yet I tell you in its day it was a piece of furniture that would have attracted attention in any drawing-room in this city. You may have it if you want it—I can't afford to repair it. Put a new bottom in her, and part of a new top, and a bit of fresh lining along the left side, and you'll find her about as comfortable as any receptacle of her species you ever tried. No thanks no, don't mention it you have been civil to me, and I would give you all the property I have got before I would seem ungrateful. Now this winding-sheet is a kind of a sweet thing in its way, if you would like to—No? Well, just as you say, but I wished to be fair and liberal there's nothing mean about me. Good-bye, friend, I must be going. I may have a good way to go tonight—don't know. I only know one thing for certain, and that is that I am on the emigrant trail now, and I'll never sleep in that crazy old cemetery again. I will travel till I find respectable quarters, if I have to hoof it to New Jersey. All the boys are going. It was decided in public conclave, last night, to emigrate, and by the time the sun rises there won't be a bone left in our old habitations. Such cemeteries may suit my surviving friends, but they do not suit the remains that have the honor to make these remarks. My opinion is the general opinion. If you doubt it, go and see how the departing ghosts upset things before they started. They were almost riotous in their demonstrations of distaste. Hello, here are some of the Bledsoes, and if you will give me a lift with this tombstone, I guess I will join company and jog along with them—mighty respectable old family, the Bledsoes, and used to always come out in six-horse hearses and all that sort of thing fifty years ago when I walked these streets in daylight. Good-bye, friend.'

And with his gravestone on his shoulder he joined the grisly procession, dragging his damaged coffin after him, for notwithstanding he pressed it upon me so earnestly, I utterly refused his hospitality. I suppose that for as much as two hours these sad outcasts went clacking by, laden with their dismal effects, and all that time I sat pitying them. One or two of the youngest and least dilapidated among them inquired about midnight trains on the railways, but the rest seemed unacquainted with that mode of travel, and merely asked about common public roads to various towns and cities, some of which are not on the map now, and vanished from it and from the earth as much as thirty years ago, and some few of them never had existed anywhere but on maps, and private ones in real-estate agencies at that. And they asked about the condition of the cemeteries in these towns and cities, and about the reputation the citizens bore as to reverence for the dead.

This whole matter interested me deeply, and likewise compelled my sympathy for these homeless ones. And it all seeming real, and I not knowing it was a dream, I mentioned to one shrouded wanderer an idea that had entered my head to publish an account of this curious and very sorrowful exodus, but said also that I could not describe it truthfully, and just as it occurred, without seeming to trifle with a grave subject and exhibit an irreverence for the dead that would shock and distress their surviving friends. But this bland and stately remnant of a former citizen leaned him far over my gate and whispered in my ear, and said:

'Do not let that disturb you. The community that can stand such graveyards as those we are emigrating from can stand anything a body can say about the neglected and forsaken dead that lie in them.'

At that very moment a cock crowed, and the weird procession vanished and left not a shred or a bone behind. I awoke, and found myself lying with my head out of the bed and 'sagging' downward considerably—a position favorable to dreaming dreams with morals in them, maybe, but not poetry.

NOTE.—The reader is assured that if the cemeteries in his town are kept in good order, this dream is not levelled at his town at all, but is leveled particularly and venomously at the next town.

5

HOW I EDITED
AN AGRICULTURAL PAPER

I did not take temporary editorship of an agricultural paper without misgivings. Neither would a landsman take command of a ship without misgivings. But I was in circumstances that made the salary an object. The regular editor of the paper was going off for a holiday, and I accepted the terms he offered, and took his place.

The sensation of being at work again was luxurious, and I wrought all the week with unflagging pleasure. We went to press, and I waited a day with some solicitude to see whether my effort was going to attract any notice. As I left the office, toward sundown, a group of men and boys at the foot of the stairs dispersed with one impulse, and gave me passageway, and I heard one or two of them say: 'That's him!' I was naturally pleased by this incident. The next morning, I found a similar group at the foot of the stairs, and scattering couples and individuals standing here and there in the street and over the way, watching me with interest. The group separated and fell back as I approached, and I heard a man say, 'Look at his eye!' I pretended not to observe the notice I was attracting, but secretly I was pleased with it, and was purposing to write an account of it to my aunt. I went up the short flight of stairs, and heard cheery voices and a ringing laugh as I drew near the door, which I opened, and caught a glimpse of two young rural-looking men, whose faces blanched and lengthened when they saw me, and then they both plunged through the window with a great crash. I was surprised.

In about half an hour, an old gentleman, with a flowing beard and a fine but rather austere face, entered, and sat down at my invitation. He seemed to have something on his mind. He took off his hat and set it on the floor, and got out of it a red silk handkerchief and a copy of our paper.

He put the paper on his lap, and while he polished his spectacles with his handkerchief he said, 'Are you the new editor?'

I said I was.

'Have you ever edited an agricultural paper before?'

'No,' I said; 'this is my first attempt.'

'Very likely. Have you had any experience in agriculture practically?'

'No; I believe I have not.'

'Some instinct told me so,' said the old gentleman, putting on his spectacles, and looking over them at me with asperity, while he folded his paper into a convenient shape. 'I wish to read you what must have made me have that instinct. It was this editorial. Listen, and see if it was you that wrote it:

"Turnips should never be pulled, it injures them. It is much better to send a boy up and let him shake the tree.'

'Now, what do you think of that? for I really suppose you wrote it?'

'Think of it? Why, I think it is good. I think it is sense. I have no doubt that every year millions and millions of bushels of turnips are spoiled in this township alone by being pulled in a half-ripe condition, when, if they had sent a boy up to shake the tree—'

'Shake your grandmother! Turnips don't grow on trees!'

'Oh, they don't, don't they? Well, who said they did? The

language was intended to be figurative, wholly figurative. Anybody that knows anything will know that I meant that the boy should shake the vine.'

Then this old person got up and tore his paper all into small shreds, and stamped on them, and broke several things with his cane, and said I did not know as much as a cow; and then went—out and banged the door after him, and, in short, acted in such a way that I fancied he was displeased about something. But not knowing what the trouble was, I could not be any help to him.

Pretty soon after this a long, cadaverous creature, with lanky locks hanging down to his shoulders, and a week's stubble bristling from the hills and valleys of his face, darted within the door, and halted, motionless, with finger on lip, and head and body bent in listening attitude. No sound was heard.

Still he listened. No sound. Then he turned the key in the door, and came elaborately tiptoeing toward me till he was within long reaching distance of me, when he stopped and, after scanning my face with intense interest for a while, drew a folded copy of our paper from his bosom, and said:

'There, you wrote that. Read it to me—quick! Relieve me. I suffer.'

I read as follows; and as the sentences fell from my lips I could see the relief come, I could see the drawn muscles relax, and the anxiety go out of the face, and rest and peace steal over the features like the merciful moonlight over a desolate landscape:

The guano is a fine bird, but great care is necessary in rearing it. It should not be imported earlier than June or later than September. In the winter it should be kept in a warm place, where it can hatch out its young.

It is evident that we are to have a backward season for grain. Therefore it will be well for the farmer to begin setting out his corn-stalks and planting his buckwheat cakes in July instead of August.

Concerning the pumpkin. This berry is a favorite with the natives of the interior of New England, who prefer it to the gooseberry for the making of fruit-cake, and who likewise give it the preference over the raspberry for feeding cows, as being more filling and fully as satisfying. The pumpkin is the only esculent of the orange family that will thrive in the North, except the gourd and one or two varieties of the squash. But the custom of planting it in the front yard with the shrubbery is fast going out of vogue, for it is now generally conceded that, the pumpkin as a shade tree is a failure.

Now, as the warm weather approaches, and the ganders begin to spawn—

The excited listener sprang toward me to shake hands, and said:

'There, there—that will do. I know I am all right now, because you have read it just as I did, word, for word. But, stranger, when I first read it this morning, I said to myself, I never, never believed it before, notwithstanding my friends kept me under watch so strict, but now I believe I am crazy; and with that I fetched a howl that you might have heard two miles, and started out to kill somebody—because, you know, I knew it would come to that sooner or later, and so I might as well begin. I read one of them paragraphs over again, so as to be certain, and then I burned my house down and started. I have crippled several people, and have got one fellow up a tree, where I can get him if I want him. But I thought I would call in here as I passed along and make the thing perfectly certain; and now it is certain, and I tell you it is lucky for the chap that is in the tree. I should have killed him sure, as I went back. Good-bye, sir, good-bye; you have taken a great load off my mind. My reason has stood the strain of one of your agricultural articles, and I know that nothing can ever unseat it now. Good-bye, sir.'

I felt a little uncomfortable about the cripplings and arsons this person had been entertaining himself with, for I could not help feeling remotely accessory to them. But these thoughts were quickly banished, for the regular editor walked in! [I thought to myself, Now if you had gone to Egypt as I recommended you to, I might have had a chance to get my hand in; but you wouldn't do it, and here you are. I sort of expected you.]

The editor was looking sad and perplexed and dejected.

He surveyed the wreck which that old rioter and those two young farmers had made, and then said 'This is a sad business—a very sad business. There is the mucilage-bottle broken, and six panes of glass, and a spittoon, and two candlesticks. But that is not the worst. The reputation of the paper is injured—and permanently, I fear. True, there never was such a call for the paper before, and it never sold such a large edition or soared to such celebrity; but does one want to be famous for lunacy, and prosper upon the infirmities of his mind? My friend, as I am an honest man, the street out here is full of people, and others are roosting on the fences, waiting to get a glimpse of you, because they think you are crazy. And well they might after reading your editorials. They are a disgrace to journalism. Why, what put it into your head that you could edit a paper of this nature? You do not seem to know the first rudiments of agriculture. You speak of a furrow and a harrow as being the same thing; you talk of the moulting season for cows; and you recommend the domestication of the pole-cat on account of its playfulness and its excellence as a ratter! Your remark that clams will lie quiet if music be played to them was superfluous—entirely superfluous. Nothing disturbs clams. Clams always lie quiet. Clams care nothing whatever about music. Ah, heavens and earth, friend! If you had made the acquiring of ignorance the study of your life, you could not have graduated with higher honor than you could today. I never saw anything like it. Your observation that the horse-chestnut as an article of commerce is steadily gaining in favor is simply calculated to destroy this journal. I want you to throw up your situation and go. I want no more holiday—I could not enjoy it, if I had it. Certainly not with you in my chair. I would always stand in dread of what you might be going to recommend next. It makes me lose all patience every time I think of your discussing oyster-beds under the head of 'Landscape Gardening.' I want you to go. Nothing on earth could persuade me to take another holiday. Oh! why didn't you tell me you didn't know anything about agriculture?'

'Tell you, you corn-stalk, you cabbage, you son of a cauliflower? It's the first time I ever heard such an unfeeling remark. I tell you I have been in the editorial business going on fourteen years, and it is the first time I ever heard of a man's having to know anything in order to edit a newspaper. You turnip! Who write the dramatic critiques for the second-rate papers? Why, a parcel of promoted shoemakers and apprentice apothecaries, who know just as much about good acting as I do about good farming and no more. Who review the books? People who never wrote one. Who do up the heavy leaders on finance? Parties who have had the largest opportunities for knowing nothing about it. Who criticize the Indian campaigns? Gentlemen who do not know a war-whoop from a wigwam, and who never have had to run a foot-race with a tomahawk, or pluck arrows out of the several members of their families to build the evening camp-fire with. Who write the temperance appeals, and clamor about the flowing bowl? Folks who will never draw another sober breath till they do it in the grave. Who edit the agricultural papers, you—yam? Men, as a general thing, who fail in the poetry line, yellow-colored novel line, sensation, drama line, city-editor line, and finally fall back on agriculture as a temporary reprieve from the poorhouse. You try to tell me anything about the newspaper business! Sir, I have been through it from Alpha to Omaha, and I tell you that the less a man knows the bigger the noise he makes and the higher the salary he commands. Heaven knows if I had but been ignorant instead of cultivated, and impudent instead of diffident, I could have made a name for myself in this cold, selfish world. I take my leave, sir. Since I have been treated as you have treated me, I am perfectly willing to go. But I have done my duty. I have fulfilled my contract as far as I was permitted to do it. I said I could make your paper of interest to all classes—and I have. I said I could run your circulation up to twenty thousand copies, and if I had had two more weeks I'd have done it. And I'd have given you the best class of readers that ever an agricultural paper had—not a farmer in it, nor a solitary individual who could tell a watermelon-tree from a peach-vine to save his life. You are the loser by this rupture, not me, Pie-plant. Adios.'

I then left.

THE £1,000,000 BANK-NOTE

When I was twenty-seven years old, I was a mining-broker's clerk in San Francisco, and an expert in all the details of stock traffic. I was alone in the world, and had nothing to depend upon but my wits and a clean reputation; but these were setting my feet in the road to eventual fortune, and I was content with the prospect.

My time was my own after the afternoon board, Saturdays, and I was accustomed to put it in on a little sail-boat on the bay. One day I ventured too far, and was carried out to sea. Just at nightfall, when hope was about gone, I was picked up by a small brig which was bound for London. It was a long and stormy voyage, and they made me work my passage without pay, as a common sailor. When I stepped ashore in London my clothes were ragged and shabby, and I had only a dollar in my pocket. This money fed and sheltered me twenty-four hours. During the next twenty-four, I went without food and shelter.

About ten o'clock on the following morning, seedy and hungry, I was dragging myself along Portland Place, when a child that was passing, towed by a nurse-maid, tossed a luscious big pear—minus one bite—into the gutter. I stopped, of course, and fastened my desiring eye on that muddy treasure. My mouth watered for it, my stomach craved it, my whole being begged for it. But every time

I made a move to get it some passing eye detected my purpose, and of course I straightened up then, and looked indifferent, and pretended that I hadn't been thinking about the pear at all. This same thing kept happening and happening, and I couldn't get the pear. I was just getting desperate enough to brave all the shame, and to seize it, when a window behind me was raised, and a gentleman spoke out of it, saying: 'Step in here, please.'

I was admitted by a gorgeous flunkey, and shown into a sumptuous room where a couple of elderly gentlemen were sitting. They sent away the servant, and made me sit down. They had just finished their breakfast, and the sight of the remains of it almost overpowered me. I could hardly keep my wits together in the presence of that food, but as I was not asked to sample it, I had to bear my trouble as best I could.

Now, something had been happening there a little before, which I did not know anything about until a good many days afterwards, but I will tell you about it now. Those two old brothers had been having a pretty hot argument a couple of days before, and had ended by agreeing to decide it by a bet, which is the English way of settling everything.

You will remember that the Bank of England once issued two notes of a million pounds each, to be used for a special purpose connected with some public transaction with a foreign country. For some reason or other only one of these had been used and canceled; the other still lay in the vaults of the Bank. Well, the brothers, chatting along, happened to get to wondering what might be the fate of a perfectly honest and intelligent stranger who should be turned adrift in London without a friend, and with no money but that million-pound bank-note, and no way to account for his being in possession of it. Brother A said he would starve to death; Brother B said he wouldn't. Brother A said he couldn't offer it at a bank or anywhere else, because he would be arrested on the spot. So they went on disputing till Brother B said he would bet twenty thousand pounds that the man would live thirty days, anyway, on that million, and keep out of jail, too. Brother A took him up. Brother B went down to the Bank and bought that note. Just like an Englishman, you see; pluck to the backbone. Then he dictated a letter, which one of his clerks wrote out in a beautiful round hand, and then the two brothers sat at the window a whole day watching for the right man to give it to.

They saw many honest faces go by that were not intelligent enough; many that were intelligent, but not honest enough; many that were both, but the possessors were not poor enough, or, if poor enough, were not strangers. There was always a defect, until I came along; but they agreed that I filled the bill all around; so they elected me unanimously, and there I was now waiting to know why I was called in. They began to ask me questions about myself, and pretty soon they had my story. Finally they told me, I would answer their purpose. I said I was sincerely glad, and asked what it was. Then one of them handed me an envelope, and said I would find the explanation inside. I was going to open it, but he said no; take it to my lodgings, and look it over carefully, and not be hasty or rash. I was puzzled, and wanted to discuss the matter a little further, but they didn't; so I took my leave, feeling hurt and insulted to be made the butt of what was apparently some kind of a practical joke, and yet obliged to put up with it, not being in circumstances to resent affronts from rich and strong folk.

I would have picked up the pear now and eaten it before all the world, but it was gone; so I had lost that by this unlucky business, and the thought of it did not soften my feeling towards those men. As soon as I was out of sight of that house I opened my envelope, and saw that it contained money! My opinion of those people changed, I can tell you! I lost not a moment, but shoved note and money into my vest pocket, and broke for the nearest cheap eating house. Well, how I did eat! When at last I couldn't hold any more, I took out my money and unfolded it, took one glimpse and nearly fainted. Five millions of dollars! Why, it made my head swim.

I must have sat there stunned and blinking at the note as much as a minute before I came rightly to myself again. The first thing I noticed, then, was the landlord. His eye was on the note, and he was petrified. He was worshiping, with all his body and soul, but he looked as if he couldn't stir hand or foot. I took my cue in a moment, and did the only rational thing there was to do. I reached the note towards him, and said, carelessly: 'Give me the change, please.'

Then he was restored to his normal condition, and made a thousand apologies for not being able to break the bill, and I couldn't get him to touch it. He wanted to look at it, and keep on looking at it; he couldn't seem to get enough of it to quench the thirst of his eye, but he shrank from touching it as if it had been something too sacred for poor common clay to handle. I said: 'I am sorry if it is an inconvenience, but I must insist. Please change it; I haven't anything else.'

But he said that wasn't any matter; he was quite willing to let the trifle stand over till another time. I said I might not be in his neighborhood again for a good while; but he said it was of no consequence, he could wait, and, moreover, I could have anything I wanted, any time I chose, and let the account run as long as I pleased. He said he hoped he wasn't afraid to trust as rich a gentleman as I was, merely because I was of a merry disposition, and chose to play larks on the public in the matter of dress. By this time another customer was entering, and the landlord hinted to me to put the monster out of sight; then he bowed me all the way to the door, and I started straight for that house and those brothers, to correct the mistake which had been made before the police should hunt me up, and help me do it. I was pretty nervous; in fact, pretty badly frightened, though, of course, I was no way in fault; but I knew men well enough to know that when they find they've given a tramp a million-pound bill, when they thought it was a one-pounder, they are in a frantic rage against him instead of quarreling with their own near-sightedness, as they ought. As I approached the house, my excitement began to abate, for all was quiet there, which made me feel pretty sure the blunder was not discovered yet. I rang. The same servant appeared. I asked for those gentlemen.

'They are gone.' This in the lofty, cold way of that fellow's tribe.

'Gone? Gone where?'

'On a journey.'

'But whereabouts?'

'To the Continent, I think.'

'The Continent?'

'Yes, sir.'

'Which way—by what route?'

'I can't say, sir.'

'When will they be back?'

'In a month, they said.'

'A month! Oh, this is awful! Give me some sort of idea, of how to get a word to them.

It's of the last importance.'

'I can't, indeed. I've no idea where they've gone, sir.'

'Then I must see some member of the family.'

'Family's away, too; been abroad months—in Egypt and India, I think.'

'Man, there's been an immense mistake made. They'll be back before night. Will you tell them I've been here, and that I will keep coming till it's all made right, and they needn't be afraid?'

'I'll tell them, if they come back, but I am not expecting them. They said you would be here in an hour to make inquiries, but I must tell you it's all right, they'll be here on time and expect you.'

So I had to give it up and go away. What a riddle it all was!

I was like to lose my mind. They would be here 'on time.' What could that mean? Oh, the letter would explain, maybe. I had forgotten the letter; I got it out and read it. This is what it said:

'You are an intelligent and honest man, as one may see by your face. We conceive you to be poor and a stranger. Enclosed you will find a sum of money. It is lent to you for thirty days, without interest. Report at this house at the end of that time. I have a bet on you. If I win it you shall have any situation that is in my gift—any, that is, that you shall be able to prove yourself familiar with and competent to fill.'

No signature, no address, no date.

Well, here was a coil to be in! You are posted on what had preceded all this, but I was not. It was just a deep, dark puzzle to me. I hadn't the least idea what the game was, nor whether harm was meant or a kindness. I went into a park, and sat down to try to think it out, and to consider what I had best do.

At the end of an hour, my reasonings had crystallized into this verdict. Maybe those men mean me well, maybe they mean me ill; no way to decide that—let it go. They've got a game, or a scheme, or an experiment, of some kind on hand; no way to determine what it is—let it go. There's a bet on me; no way to find out what it is—let it go. That disposes of the indeterminable quantities; the remainder of the matter is tangible, solid, and may be classed and labeled with certainty. If I ask the Bank of England to place this bill to the credit of the man it belongs to, they'll do it, for they know him, although I don't; but they will ask me how I came in possession of it, and if I tell the truth, they'll put me in the asylum, naturally, and a lie will land me in jail. The same result would follow if I tried to bank the bill anywhere or to borrow money on it. I have got to carry this immense burden around until those men come back, whether I want to or not. It is useless to me, as useless as a handful of ashes, and yet I must take care of it, and watch over it, while I beg my living. I couldn't give it away, if I should try, for neither honest citizen nor highwayman would accept it or meddle with it for anything. Those brothers are safe. Even if I lose their bill, or burn it, they are still safe, because they can stop payment, and the Bank will make them whole; but meantime I've got to do a month's suffering without wages or profit—unless I help win that bet, whatever it may be, and get that situation that I am promised. I should like to get that; men of their sort have situations in their gift that are worth having.

I got to thinking a good deal about that situation. My hopes began to rise high. Without doubt the salary would be large. It would begin in a month; after that I should be all right. Pretty soon I was feeling first-rate. By this time, I was tramping the streets again. The sight of a tailor-shop gave me a sharp longing to shed my rags, and to clothe myself decently once more. Could I afford it? No; I had nothing in the world but a million pounds. So I forced myself to go on by. But soon I was drifting back again. The temptation persecuted me cruelly. I must have passed that shop back and forth six times during that manful struggle. At last I gave in; I had to. I asked if they had a misfit suit that had been thrown on their hands. The fellow I spoke to nodded his head towards another fellow, and gave me no answer. I went to the indicated fellow, and he indicated another fellow with his head, and no words. I went to him, and he said: ' 'Tend to you presently.'

I waited till he was done with what he was at, then he took me into a back room, and overhauled a pile of rejected suits, and selected the rattiest one for me. I put it on. It didn't fit, and wasn't in any way attractive, but it was new, and I was anxious to have it; so I didn't find any fault, but said, with some diffidence: 'It would be an accommodation to me if you could wait some days for the money. I haven't any small change about me.'

The fellow worked up a most sarcastic expression of countenance, and said: 'Oh, you haven't? Well, of course, I didn't expect it. I'd only expect gentlemen like you to carry large change.'

I was nettled, and said: 'My friend, you shouldn't judge a stranger always by the clothes he wears. I am quite able to pay for this suit; I simply didn't wish to put you to the trouble of changing a large note.'

He modified his style a little at that, and said, though still with something of an air: 'I didn't mean any particular harm, but as long as rebukes are going, I might say it wasn't quite your affair to jump to the conclusion that we couldn't change any note that you might happen to be carrying around. On the contrary, we can.'

I handed the note to him, and said: 'Oh, very well; I apologize.'

He received it with a smile, one of those large smiles which goes all around over, and has folds in it, and wrinkles, and spirals, and looks like the place where you have thrown a brick in a pond; and then in the act of his taking a glimpse of the bill this smile froze solid, and turned yellow, and looked like those wavy, wormy spreads of lava which you find hardened on little levels on the side of Vesuvius. I never before saw a smile caught like that, and perpetuated. The man stood there holding the bill, and looking like that, and the proprietor hustled up to see what was the matter, and said, briskly: 'Well, what's up? what's the trouble? what's wanting?'

I said: 'There isn't any trouble. I'm waiting for my change.'

'Come, come; get him his change, Tod; get him his change.'

Tod retorted: 'Get him his change! It's easy to say, sir; but look at the bill yourself.'

The proprietor took a look, gave a low, eloquent whistle, then made a dive for the pile of rejected clothing, and began to snatch it this way and that, talking all the time excitedly, and as if to himself: 'Sell an eccentric millionaire such an unspeakable suit as that! Tod's a fool—a born fool. Always doing something like this. Drives every millionaire away from this place, because he can't tell a millionaire from a tramp, and never could. Ah, here's the thing I am after. Please get those things off, sir, and throw them in the fire. Do me the favor to put on this shirt and this suit; it's just the thing, the very thing—plain, rich, modest, and just ducally nobby; made to order for a foreign prince—you may know him, sir, his Serene Highness the Hospodar of Halifax; had to leave it with us and take a mourning-suit because his mother was going to die—which she didn't. But that's all right; we can't always have things the way we—that is, the way they—there! trousers all right, they fit you to a charm, sir; now the waistcoat; aha, right again! now the coat—Lord! look at that, now! Perfect—the whole thing! I never saw such a triumph in all my experience.' I expressed my satisfaction.

'Quite right, sir, quite right; it'll do for a makeshift, I'm bound to say. But wait till you see what we'll get up for you on your own measure. Come, Tod, book and pen; get at it. Length of leg, 32"— and so on. Before I could get in a word he had measured me, and was giving orders for dress-suits, morning suits, shirts, and all sorts of things. When I got a chance I said: 'But, my dear sir, I can't give these orders, unless you can wait indefinitely, or change the bill.'

'Indefinitely! It's a weak word, sir, a weak word. Eternally— that's the word, sir. Tod, rush these things through, and send them to the gentleman's address without any waste of time. Let the minor customers wait. Set down the gentleman's address and—'

'I'm changing my quarters. I will drop in and leave the new address.'

'Quite right, sir, quite right. One moment—let me show you out, sir. There—good day, sir, good day.'

Well, don't you see what was bound to happen? I drifted naturally into buying whatever I wanted, and asking for change. Within a week, I was sumptuously equipped with all needful comforts and luxuries, and was housed in an expensive private hotel in Hanover Square. I took my dinners there, but for breakfast I stuck by Harris's humble feeding house, where I had got my first meal on my million-pound bill. I was the making of Harris. The fact had gone all abroad that the foreign crank who carried million-pound bills in his vest pocket was the patron saint of the place. That was enough. From being a poor, struggling, little hand-to-mouth enterprise, it had become celebrated, and overcrowded with customers. Harris was so grateful that he forced loans upon me, and would not be denied; and so, pauper as I was, I had money to spend, and was living like the rich and the great. I judged that there was going to be a crash by and by, but I was in now and must swim across or drown. You see there was just that element of impending disaster to give a serious side, a sober side, yes, a tragic side, to a state of things which would otherwise have been purely ridiculous. In the night, in the dark, the tragedy part was always to the front, and always warning, always threatening; and so I moaned and tossed, and sleep was hard to find. But in the cheerful daylight, the tragedy element faded out and disappeared, and I walked on air, and was happy to giddiness, to intoxication, you may say.

And it was natural; for I had become one of the notorieties of the metropolis of the world, and it turned my head, not just a little, but a good deal. You could not take up a newspaper, English, Scotch, or Irish, without finding in it one or more references to the 'vest-pocket million-pounder' and his latest doings and saying. At first, in these mentions, I was at the bottom of the personal-gossip column; next, I was listed above the knights, next above the baronets, next above the barons, and so on, and so on, climbing steadily, as my notoriety augmented, until I reached the highest altitude possible, and there I remained, taking precedence of all dukes not royal, and of all ecclesiastics except the primate of all England. But mind, this was not fame; as yet I had achieved only notoriety. Then came the climaxing stroke—the accolade, so to speak—which in a single instant transmuted the perishable dross of notoriety into the enduring gold of fame: Punch caricatured me! Yes, I was a made man now; my place was established. I might be joked about still, but reverently, not hilariously, not rudely; I could be smiled at, but not laughed at. The time for that had gone by. Punch pictured me all a-flutter with rags, dickering with a beef-eater for the Tower of London. Well, you can imagine how it was with a young fellow who had never been taken notice of before, and now all of a sudden couldn't say a thing that wasn't taken up and repeated everywhere; couldn't stir abroad without constantly overhearing the remark flying from lip to lip, 'There he goes; that's him!' couldn't take his breakfast without a crowd to look on; couldn't appear in an operabox without concentrating there the fire of a thousand lorgnettes. Why, I just swam in glory all day long—that is the amount of it.

You know, I even kept my old suit of rags, and every now and then appeared in them, so as to have the old pleasure of buying trifles, and being insulted, and then shooting the scoffer dead with the million-pound bill. But I couldn't keep that up. The illustrated papers made the outfit so familiar that when I went out in it I was at once recognized and followed by a crowd, and if I attempted a purchase the man would offer me his whole shop on credit before I could pull my note on him.

About the tenth day of my fame, I went to fulfil my duty to my flag by paying my respects to the American minister. He received me with the enthusiasm proper in my case, upbraided me for being so tardy in my duty, and said that there was only one way to get his forgiveness, and that was to take the seat at his dinner-party that night made vacant by the illness of one of his guests. I said I would, and we got to talking. It turned out that he and my father had been schoolmates in boyhood, Yale students together later, and always warm friends up to my father's death. So then he required me to put in at his house all the odd time I might have to spare, and I was very willing, of course.

In fact, I was more than willing; I was glad. When the crash should come, he might somehow be able to save me from total destruction; I didn't know how, but he might think of a way, maybe. I couldn't venture to unbosom myself to him at this late date, a thing which I would have been quick to do in the beginning of this awful career of mine in London. No, I couldn't venture it now; I was in too deep; that is, too deep for me to be risking revelations to so new a friend, though not clear beyond my depth, as I looked at it. Because, you see, with all my borrowing, I was carefully keeping within my means—I mean within my salary. Of course, I couldn't know what my salary was going to be, but I had a good enough basis for an estimate in the fact, that if I won the bet I was to have choice of any situation in that rich old gentleman's gift provided I was competent—and I should certainly prove competent; I hadn't any doubt about that. And as to the bet, I wasn't worrying about that; I had always been lucky. Now my estimate of the salary was six hundred to a thousand a year; say, six hundred for the first year, and so on up year by year, till I struck the upper figure by proved merit. At present, I was only in debt for my first year's salary. Everybody had been trying to lend me money, but I had fought off the most of them on one pretext or another; so this indebtedness represented only £300 borrowed money, the other £300 represented my keep and my purchases. I believed my second year's salary would carry me through the rest of the month if I went on being cautious and economical, and I intended to look sharply out for that. My month ended, my employer back from his journey, I should be all right once more, for I should at once divide the two years' salary among my creditors by assignment, and get right down to my work.

It was a lovely dinner-party of fourteen. The Duke and Duchess of Shoreditch, and their daughter the Lady Anne-Grace-Eleanor-Celeste-and-so-forth-and-so-forth-de-Bohun, the Earl and Countess of Newgate, Viscount Cheapside, Lord and Lady Blatherskite, some untitled people of both sexes, the minister and his wife and daughter, and his daughter's visiting friend, an English girl of twenty-two, named Portia Langham, whom I fell in love with in two minutes, and she with me—I could see it without glasses. There was still another guest, an American—but I am a little ahead of my story. While the people were still in the drawing-room, whetting up for dinner, and coldly inspecting the late comers, the servant announced: 'Mr. Lloyd Hastings.'

The moment the usual civilities were over, Hastings caught sight of me, and came straight with cordially outstretched hand; then stopped short when about to shake, and said, with an embarrassed look: 'I beg your pardon, sir, I thought I knew you.' 'Why, you do know me, old fellow.' 'No. Are you the—the—'

'Vest-pocket monster? I am, indeed. Don't be afraid to call me by my nickname; I'm used to it.'

'Well, well, well, this is a surprise. Once or twice I've seen your own name coupled with the nickname, but it never occurred to me that you could be the Henry Adams referred to. Why, it isn't six months since you were clerking away for Blake Hopkins in Frisco on a salary, and sitting up nights on an extra allowance, helping me arrange and verify the Gould and Curry Extension papers and statistics. The idea of your being in London, and a vast millionaire, and a colossal celebrity! Why, it's the Arabian Nights come again. Man, I can't take it in at all; can't realize it; give me time to settle the whirl in my head.'

'The fact is, Lloyd, you are no worse off than I am. I can't realize it myself.'

'Dear me, it is stunning, now isn't it? Why, it's just three months today since we went to the Miners' restaurant—'

'No; the What Cheer.'

'Right, it was the What Cheer; went there at two in the morning, and had a chop and coffee after a hard six-hours grind over those Extension papers, and I tried to persuade you to come to London with me, and offered to get leave of absence for you and pay all your expenses, and give you something over if I succeeded in making the sale; and you would not listen to me, said I wouldn't succeed, and you couldn't afford to lose the run of business and be no end of time getting the hang of things again when you got back home. And yet here you are. How odd it all is! How did you happen to come, and whatever did give you this incredible start?'

'Oh, just an accident. It's a long story—a romance, a body may say. I'll tell you all about it, but not now.'

'When?'

'The end of this month.'

'That's more than a fortnight yet. It's too much of a strain on a person's curiosity. Make it a week.'

'I can't. You'll know why, by and by. But how's the trade getting along?'

His cheerfulness vanished like a breath, and he said with a sigh: 'You were a true prophet, Hal, a true prophet. I wish I hadn't come. I don't want to talk about it.'

'But you must. You must come and stop with me tonight, when we leave here, and tell me all about it.'

'Oh, may I? Are you in earnest?' and the water showed in his eyes.

'Yes; I want to hear the whole story, every word.'

'I'm so grateful! Just to find a human interest once more, in some voice and in some eye, in me and affairs of mine, after what I've been through here—lord! I could go down on my knees for it!'

He gripped my hand hard, and braced up, and was all right and lively after that for the dinner—which didn't come off. No; the usual thing happened, the thing that is always happening under that vicious and aggravating English system—the matter of precedence couldn't be settled, and so there was no dinner. Englishmen always eat dinner before they go out to dinner, because they know the risks they are running; but nobody ever warns the stranger, and so he walks placidly into trap. Of course, nobody was hurt this time, because we had all been to dinner, none of us being novices excepting Hastings, and he having been informed by the minister at the time that he invited him that in deference to the English custom he had not provided any dinner. Everybody took a lady and processioned down to the dining-room, because it is usual to go through the motions; but there the dispute began. The Duke of Shoreditch wanted to take precedence, and sit at the head of the table, holding that he outranked a minister who represented merely a nation and not a monarch; but I stood for my rights, and refused to yield. In the gossip column, I ranked all dukes not royal, and said so, and claimed precedence of this one. It couldn't be settled, of course, struggle as we might and did, he finally (and injudiciously) trying to play birth and antiquity, and I 'seeing' his Conqueror and 'raising' him with Adam, whose direct posterity I was, as shown by my name, while he was of a collateral branch, as shown by his, and by his recent Norman origin; so we all processioned back to the drawing-room again and had a perpendicular lunch—plate of sardines and a strawberry, and you group yourself and stand up and eat it. Here the religion of precedence is not so strenuous; the two persons of highest rank chuck up a shilling, the one that wins has first go at his strawberry, and the loser gets the shilling. The next two chuck up, then the next two, and so on. After refreshment, tables were brought, and we all played cribbage, sixpence a game. The English never play any game for amusement. If they can't make something or lose something—they don't care which—they won't play.

We had a lovely time; certainly two of us had, Miss Langham and I. I was so bewitched with her that I couldn't count my hands if they went above a double sequence; and when I struck home I never discovered it, and started up the outside row again, and would have lost the game every time, only the girl did the same, she being in just my condition, you see; and consequently neither of us ever got out, or cared to wonder why we didn't; we only just knew we were happy, and didn't wish to know anything else, and didn't want to be interrupted. And I told her—I did, indeed—told her I loved her; and she—well, she blushed till her hair turned red, but she liked it; she said she did. Oh, there was never such an evening! Every time I pegged I put on a postscript; every time she pegged she acknowledged receipt of it, counting the hands the same. Why, I couldn't even say 'Two for his heels' without adding, 'My, how sweet you do look!' and she would say, 'Fifteen two, fifteen four, fifteen six, and a pair are eight, and eight are sixteen—do you think so?'—peeping out aslant from under her lashes, you know, so sweet and cunning. Oh, it was just too-too!

Well, I was perfectly honest and square with her; told her I hadn't a cent in the world but just the million-pound note she'd heard so much talk about, and it didn't belong to me, and that started her curiosity; and then I talked low, and told her the whole history right from the start, and it nearly killed her laughing. What in the nation she could find to laugh about I couldn't see, but there it was; every half-minute some new detail would fetch her, and I would have to stop as much as a minute and a half to give her a chance to settle down again. Why, she laughed herself lame— she did, indeed; I never saw anything like it. I mean I never saw a painful story—a story of a person's troubles and worries and fears—produce just that kind of effect before. So I loved her all the more, seeing she could be so cheerful when there wasn't anything to be cheerful about; for I might soon need that kind of wife, you know, the way things looked. Of course, I told her we should have to wait a couple of years, till I could catch up on my salary; but she didn't mind that, only she hoped I would be as careful as possible in the matter of expenses, and not let them run the least risk of trenching on our third year's pay. Then she began to get a little worried, and wondered if we were making any mistake, and starting the salary on a higher figure for the first year than I could get. This was good sense, and it made me feel a little less confident than I had been feeling before; but it gave me a good business idea, and I brought it frankly out.

'Portia, dear, would you mind going with me that day, when I confront those old gentlemen?'

She shrank a little, but said:

'No; if my being with you would help hearten you. But— would it be quite proper, do you think?'

'No, I don't know that it would—in fact, I'm afraid it wouldn't; but, you see, there's so much dependent upon it that—'

'Then I'll go anyway, proper or improper,' she said, with a beautiful and generous enthusiasm. 'Oh, I shall be so happy to think I'm helping!'

'Helping, dear? Why, you'll be doing it all. You're so beautiful and so lovely and so winning, that with you there I can pile our salary up till I break those good old fellows, and they'll never have the heart to struggle.'

Sho! you should have seen the rich blood mount, and her happy eyes shine!

'You wicked flatterer! There isn't a word of truth in what you say, but still I'll go with you. Maybe it will teach you not to expect other people to look with your eyes.'

Were my doubts dissipated? Was my confidence restored? You may judge by this fact: privately I raised my salary to twelve hundred the first year on the spot. But I didn't tell her; I saved it for a surprise.

All the way home I was in the clouds, Hastings talking, I not hearing a word. When he and I entered my parlor, he brought me to myself with his fervent appreciations of my manifold comforts and luxuries.

'Let me just stand here a little and look my fill. Dear me! it's a palace—it's just a palace! And in it everything a body could desire, including cosy coal fire and supper standing ready. Henry, it doesn't merely make me realize how rich you are; it makes me realize, to the bone, to the marrow, how poor I am —how poor I am, and how miserable, how defeated, routed, annihilated!'

Plague take it! this language gave me the cold shudders. It scared me broad awake, and made me comprehend that I was standing on a halfinch crust, with a crater underneath. I didn't know I had been dreaming—that is, I hadn't been allowing myself to know it for a while back; but now—oh, dear! Deep in debt, not a cent in the world, a lovely girl's happiness or woe in my hands, and nothing in front of me but a salary which might never—oh, would never—materialize! Oh, oh, oh! I am ruined past hope! nothing can save me!

'Henry, the mere unconsidered drippings of your daily income would—'

'Oh, my daily income! Here, down with this hot Scotch, and cheer up your soul. Here's with you! Or, no—you're hungry; sit down and—'

'Not a bite for me; I'm past it. I can't eat, these days; but I'll drink with you till I drop. Come!'

'Barrel for barrel, I'm with you! Ready? Here we go! Now, then, Lloyd, unreel your story while I brew.'

'Unreel it? What, again?'

'Again? What do you mean by that?'

'Why, I mean do you want to hear it over again?'

'Do I want to hear it over again? This is a puzzler. Wait; don't take any more of that liquid. You don't need it.'

'Look here, Henry, you alarm me. Didn't I tell you the whole story on the way here?'

'You?'

'Yes, I.'

'I'll be hanged if I heard a word of it.'

'Henry, this is a serious thing. It troubles me. What did you take up yonder at the minister's?'

Then it all flashed on me, and I owned up like a man.

'I took the dearest girl in this world—prisoner!'

So then he came with a rush, and we shook, and shook, and

shook till our hands ached; and he didn't blame me for not having heard a word of a story which had lasted while we walked three miles. He just sat down then, like the patient, good fellow he was, and told it all over again. Synopsized, it amounted to this: He had come to England with what he thought was a grand opportunity; he had an 'option' to sell the Gould and Curry Extension for the 'locators' of it, and keep all he could get over a million dollars. He had worked hard, had pulled every wire he knew of, had left no honest expedient untried, had spent nearly all the money he had in the world, had not been able to get a solitary capitalist to listen to him, and his option would run out at the end of the month. In a word, he was ruined. Then he jumped up and cried out:

'Henry, you can save me! You can save me, and you're the only man in the universe that can. Will you do it? Won't you do it?'

'Tell me how. Speak out, my boy.'

'Give me a million and my passage home for my 'option'! Don't, don't refuse!'

I was in a kind of agony. I was right on the point of coming out with the words, 'Lloyd, I'm a pauper myself—absolutely penniless, and in debt!' But a white-hot idea came flaming through my head, and I gripped my jaws together, and calmed myself down till I was as cold as a capitalist. Then I said, in a commercial and self-possessed way: 'I will save you, Lloyd—'

'Then I'm already saved! God be merciful to you forever! If ever I—'

'Let me finish, Lloyd. I will save you, but not in that way; for that would not be fair to you, after your hard work, and the risks you've run. I don't need to buy mines; I can keep my capital moving, in a commercial center like London, without that; it's what I'm at, all the time; but here is what I'll do. I know all about that mine, of course; I know its immense value, and can swear to it if anybody wishes it. You shall sell out inside of the fortnight for three millions cash, using my name freely, and we'll divide, share and share alike.'

Do you know, he would have danced the furniture to kindling-wood in his insane joy, and broken everything on the place, if I hadn't tripped him up and tied him.

Then he lay there, perfectly happy, saying:

'I may use your name! Your name—think of it! Man, they'll flock in droves, these rich Londoners; they'll fight for that stock! I'm a made man, I'm a made man forever, and I'll never forget you as long as I live!'

In less than twenty-four hours, London was abuzz! I hadn't anything to do, day after day, but sit at home, and say to all comers:

'Yes; I told him to refer to me. I know the man, and I know the mine. His character is above reproach, and the mine is worth far more than he asks for it.'

Meantime, I spent all my evenings at the minister's with Portia. I didn't say a word to her about the mine; I saved it for a surprise. We talked salary; never anything but salary and love; sometimes love, sometimes salary, sometimes love and salary together. And my! the interest the minister's wife and daughter took in our little affair, and the endless ingenuities they invented to save us from interruption, and to keep the minister in the dark and unsuspicious—well, it was just lovely of them!

When the month was up at last, I had a million dollars to my credit in the London and County Bank, and Hastings was fixed in the same way. Dressed at my level best, I drove by the house in Portland Place, judged by the look of things that my birds were home again, went on towards the minister's and got my precious, and we started back, talking salary with all our might. She was so excited and anxious that it made her just intolerably beautiful. I said:

'Dearie, the way you're looking it's a crime to strike for a salary a single penny under three thousand a year.'

'Henry, Henry, you'll ruin us!'

'Don't you be afraid. Just keep up those looks, and trust to me. It'll all come out right.'

So, as it turned out, I had to keep bolstering up her courage all the way. She kept pleading with me, and saying:

'Oh, please remember that if we ask for too much we may get no salary at all; and then what will become of us, with no way in the world to earn our living?'

We were ushered in, by that same servant, and there they were, the two old gentlemen. Of course, they were surprised to see that wonderful creature with me, but I said: 'It's all right, gentlemen; she is my future stay and helpmate.'

And I introduced them to her, and called them by name. It didn't surprise them; they knew I would know enough to consult the directory. They seated us, and were very polite to me, and very solicitous to relieve her from embarrassment, and put her as much at her ease as they could. Then I said: 'Gentlemen, I am ready to report.'

'We are glad to hear it,' said my man, 'for now we can decide the bet which my brother Abel and I made. If you have won for me, you shall have any situation in my gift. Have you the million-pound note?'

'Here it is, sir,' and I handed it to him.

'I've won!' he shouted, and slapped Abel on the back. 'Now what do you say, brother?'

'I say he did survive, and I've lost twenty thousand pounds. I never would have believed it.'

'I've a further report to make,' I said, 'and a pretty long one. I want you to let me come soon, and detail my whole month's history; and I promise you it's worth hearing. Meantime, take a look at that.'

'What, man! Certificate of deposit for £200,000. Is it yours?'

'Mine. I earned it by thirty days' judicious use of that little loan you let me have. And the only use I made of it was to buy trifles and offer the bill in change.'

'Come, this is astonishing! It's incredible, man!'

'Never mind, I'll prove it. Don't take my word unsupported.'

But now Portia's turn was come to be surprised. Her eyes were spread wide, and she said:

'Henry, is that really your money? Have you been fibbing to me?'

'I have, indeed, dearie. But you'll forgive me, I know.'

She put up an arch pout, and said: 'Don't you be so sure. You are a naughty thing to deceive me so!'

'Oh, you'll get over it, sweetheart, you'll get over it; it was only fun, you know. Come, let's be going.'

'But wait, wait! The situation, you know. I want to give you the situation,' said my man.

'Well,' I said, 'I'm just as grateful as I can be, but really I don't want one.'

'But you can have the very choicest one in my gift.'

'Thanks again, with all my heart; but I don't even want that one.'

'Henry, I'm ashamed of you. You don't half thank the good gentleman. May I do it for you?'

'Indeed, you shall, dear, if you can improve it. Let us see you try.'

She walked to my man, got up in his lap, put her arm round his neck, and kissed him right on the mouth. Then the two old gentlemen shouted with laughter, but I was dumfounded, just petrified, as you may say. Portia said:

'Papa, he has said you haven't a situation in your gift that he'd take; and I feel just as hurt as—'

'My darling, is that your papa?'

'Yes; he's my step-papa, and the dearest one that ever was. You understand now, don't you, why I was able to laugh when you told me at the minister's, not knowing my relationships, what trouble and worry papa's and Uncle Abel's scheme was giving you?'

Of course, I spoke right up now, without any fooling, and went straight to the point.

'Oh, my dearest dear sir, I want to take back what I said. You have got a situation open that I want.'

'Name it.'

'Son-in-law.'

'Well, well, well! But you know, if you haven't ever served in that capacity, you, of course, can't furnish recommendations of a sort to satisfy the conditions of the contract, and so—'

'Try me—oh, do, I beg of you! Only just try me thirty or forty years, and if—'

'Oh, well, all right; it's but a little thing to ask, take her along.'

Happy, we two? There are not words enough in the unabridged to describe it. And when London got the whole history, a day or two later, of my month's adventures with that bank-note, and how they ended, did London talk, and have a good time? Yes.

My Portia's papa took that friendly and hospitable bill back to the Bank of England and cashed it; then the Bank canceled it and made him a present of it, and he gave it to us at our wedding, and it has always hung in its frame in the sacredest place in our home ever since. For it gave me my Portia. But for it I could not have remained in London, would not have appeared at the minister's, never should have met her. And so I always say, 'Yes, it's a million-pounder, as you see; but it never made but one purchase in its life, and then got the article for only about a tenth part of its value.'

THE INVALID'S STORY

I seem sixty and married, but these effects are due to my condition and sufferings, for I am a bachelor, and only forty-one. It will be hard for you to believe that I, who am now but a shadow, was a hale, hearty man two short years ago, a man of iron, a very athlete!—yet such is the simple truth. But stranger still than this fact is the way in which I lost my health. I lost it through helping to take care of a box of guns on a two-hundred-mile railway journey one winter's night. It is the actual truth, and I will tell you about it.

I belong in Cleveland, Ohio. One winter's night, two years ago, I reached home just after dark, in a driving snow-storm, and the first thing I heard when I entered the house was that my dearest boyhood friend and schoolmate, John B. Hackett, had died the day before, and that his last utterance had been a desire that I would take his remains home to his poor old father and mother in Wisconsin. I was greatly shocked and grieved, but there was no time to waste in emotions; I must start at once. I took the card, marked 'Deacon Levi Hackett, Bethlehem, Wisconsin,' and hurried off through the whistling storm to the railway station. Arrived there, I found the long white-pine box which had been described to me; I fastened the card to it with some tacks, saw it put safely aboard the express car, and then ran into the eating-room to provide myself with a sandwich and some cigars.

When I returned, presently, there was my coffin-box back again, apparently, and a young fellow examining around it, with a card in his hands, and some tacks and a hammer! I was astonished and puzzled. He began to nail on his card, and I rushed out to the express car, in a good deal of a state of mind, to ask for an explanation. But no—there was my box, all right, in the express car; it hadn't been disturbed. [The fact is that without my suspecting it a prodigious mistake had been made. I was carrying off a box of guns which that young fellow had come to the station to ship to a rifle company in Peoria, Illinois, and he had got my corpse!] Just then the conductor sung out 'All aboard,' and I jumped into the express car and got a comfortable seat on a bale of buckets. The expressman was there, hard at work,—a plain man of fifty, with a simple, honest, good- natured face, and a breezy, practical heartiness in his general style. As the train moved off, a stranger skipped into the car and set a package of peculiarly mature and capable Limburger cheese on one end of my coffin-box—I mean my box of guns. That is to say, I know now that it was Limburger cheese, but at that time I never had heard of the article in my life, and of course was wholly ignorant of its character. Well, we sped through the wild night, the bitter storm raged on, a cheerless misery stole over me, my heart went down, down, down! The old expressman made a brisk remark or two about the tempest and the arctic weather, slammed his sliding doors to, and bolted them, closed his window down tight, and then went bustling around, here and there and yonder, setting things to right, and all the time contentedly humming 'Sweet By and By,' in a low tone, and flatting a good deal. Presently, I began to detect a most evil and searching odor stealing about on the frozen air. This depressed my spirits still more, because of course I attributed it to my poor departed friend. There was something infinitely saddening about his calling himself to my remembrance in this dumb pathetic way, so it was hard to keep the tears back. Moreover, it distressed me on account of the old expressman, who, I was afraid, might notice it. However, he went humming tranquilly on, and gave no sign; and for this I was grateful. Grateful, yes, but still uneasy; and soon I began to feel more and more uneasy every minute, for every minute that went by that odor thickened up the more, and got to be more and more gamey and hard to stand. Presently, having got things arranged to his satisfaction, the expressman got some wood and made up a tremendous fire in his stove.

This distressed me more than I can tell, for I could not but feel that it was a mistake. I was sure that the effect would be deleterious upon my poor departed friend. Thompson—the expressman's name was Thompson, as I found out in the course of the night—now went poking around his car, stopping up whatever stray cracks he could find, remarking that it didn't make any difference what kind of a night it was outside, he calculated to make us comfortable, anyway. I said nothing, but I believed he was not choosing the right way. Meantime, he was humming to himself just as before; and meantime, too, the stove was getting hotter and hotter, and the place closer and closer. I felt myself growing pale and qualmish, but grieved in silence and said nothing.

Soon I noticed that the 'Sweet By and By' was gradually fading out; next it ceased altogether, and there was an ominous stillness. After a few moments, Thompson said, 'Pfew! I reckon it ain't no cinnamon 't I've loaded up thish-yer stove with!'

He gasped once or twice, then moved toward the cof—gun-box, stood over that Limburger cheese part of a moment, then came back and sat down near me, looking a good deal impressed. After a contemplative pause, he said, indicating the box with a gesture,

'Friend of yours?'

'Yes,' I said with a sigh.

'He's pretty ripe, ain't he!'

Nothing further was said for perhaps a couple of minutes,

each being busy with his own thoughts; then Thompson said, in a low, awed voice,

'Sometimes it's uncertain whether they're really gone or not,—seem gone, you know—body warm, joints limber—and so, although you think they're gone, you don't really know. I've had cases in my car. It's perfectly awful, because you don't know what minute they'll rise up and look at you!' Then, after a pause, and slightly lifting his elbow toward the box,— 'But he ain't in no trance! No, sir, I go bail for him!'

We sat some time, in meditative silence, listening to the wind and the roar of the train; then Thompson said, with a good deal of feeling,

'Well-a-well, we've all got to go, they ain't no getting around it. Man that is born of woman is of few days and far between, as Scriptur' says. Yes, you look at it any way you want to, it's awful solemn and cur'us: they ain't nobody can get around it; all's got to go—just everybody, as you may say. One day you're hearty and strong'—here he scrambled to his feet and broke a pane and stretched his nose out at it a moment or two, then sat down again while I struggled up and thrust my nose out at the same place, and this we kept on doing every now and then—' and next day he's cut down like the grass, and the places which knowed him then knows him no more forever, as Scriptur' says. Yes'ndeedy, it's awful solemn and cur'us; but we've all got to go, one time or another; they ain't no getting around it.'

There was another long pause; then,—

'What did he die of?'

I said I didn't know.

'How long has he ben dead?'

It seemed judicious to enlarge the facts to fit the probabilities; so I said,

'Two or three days.'

But it did no good; for Thompson received it with an injured look which plainly said, 'Two or three years, you mean.' Then he went right along, placidly ignoring my statement, and gave his views at considerable length upon the unwisdom of putting off burials too long. Then he lounged off toward the box, stood a moment, then came back on a sharp trot and visited the broken pane, observing,

"Twould 'a' ben a dum sight better, all around, if they'd started him along last summer.'

Thompson sat down and buried his face in his red silk handkerchief, and began to slowly sway and rock his body like one who is doing his best to endure the almost unendurable. By this time the fragrance—if you may call it fragrance—was just about suffocating, as near as you can come at it. Thompson's face was turning gray; I knew mine hadn't any color left in it. By and by Thompson rested his forehead in his left hand, with his elbow on his knee, and sort of waved his red handkerchief towards the box with his other hand, and said,—

'I've carried a many a one of 'em,—some of 'em considerable overdue, too,—but, lordy, he just lays over 'em all!—and does it easy Cap., they was heliotrope to HIM!'

This recognition of my poor friend gratified me, in spite of the sad circumstances, because it had so much the sound of a compliment.

Pretty soon it was plain that something had got to be done. I suggested cigars. Thompson thought it was a good idea. He said,

'Likely it'll modify him some.'

We puffed gingerly along for a while, and tried hard to imagine that things were improved. But it wasn't any use. Before very long, and without any consultation, both cigars were quietly dropped from our nerveless fingers at the same moment. Thompson said, with a sigh,

'No, Cap., it don't modify him worth a cent. Fact is, it makes him worse, because it appears to stir up his ambition. What do you reckon we better do, now?'

I was not able to suggest anything; indeed, I had to be swallowing and swallowing, all the time, and did not like to trust myself to speak. Thompson fell to maundering, in a desultory and low-spirited way, about the miserable experiences of this night; and he got to referring to my poor friend by various titles,— sometimes military ones, sometimes civil ones; and I noticed that as fast as my poor friend's effectiveness grew, Thompson promoted him accordingly,—gave him a bigger title. Finally he said,

'I've got an idea. Suppos' n we buckle down to it and give the Colonel a bit of a shove towards t'other end of the car? —about ten foot, say. He wouldn't have so much influence, then, don't you reckon?'

I said it was a good scheme. So we took in a good fresh breath at the broken pane, calculating to hold it till we got through; then we went there and bent over that deadly cheese and took a grip on the box. Thompson nodded 'All ready,' and then we threw ourselves forward with all our might; but Thompson slipped, and slumped down with his nose on the cheese, and his breath got loose. He gagged and gasped, and floundered up and made a break for the door, pawing the air and saying hoarsely, 'Don't hender me! —gimme the road! I'm dying; gimme the road!' Out on the cold platform I sat down and held his head a while, and he revived. Presently he said,

'Do you reckon we started the Gen'rul any?'

I said no; we hadn't budged him.

'Well, then, that idea's up the flume. We got to think up something else. He's suited wher' he is, I reckon; and if that's the way he feels about it, and has made up his mind that he don't wish to be disturbed, you bet he's going to have his own way in the business. Yes, better leave him right wher' he is, long as he wants it so; because he holds all the trumps, don't you know, and so it stands to reason that the man that lays out to alter his plans for him is going to get left.'

But we couldn't stay out there in that mad storm; we should have frozen to death. So we went in again and shut the door, and began to suffer once more and take turns at the break in the window. By and by, as we were starting away from a station where we had stopped a moment Thompson. pranced in cheerily, and exclaimed, 'we're all right, now! I reckon we've got the Commodore this time. I judge, I've got the stuff here that'll take the tuck out of him.'

It was carbolic acid. He had a carboy of it. He sprinkled it all around everywhere; in fact he drenched everything with it, rifle-box, cheese and all. Then we sat down, feeling pretty hopeful. But it wasn't for long. You see the two perfumes began to mix, and then—well, pretty soon we made a break for the door; and out there Thompson swabbed his face with his bandanna and said in a kind of disheartened way,

'It ain't no use. We can't buck agin him. He just utilizes everything we put up to modify him with, and gives it his own flavor and plays it back on us. Why, Cap., don't you know, it's as much as a hundred times worse in there now than it was when he first got a-going. I never did see one of 'em warm up to his work so, and take such a dumnation interest in it. No, sir, I never did, as long as I've ben on the road; and I've carried a many a one of 'em, as I was telling you.'

We went in again after we were frozen pretty stiff; but my, we couldn't stay in, now. So we just waltzed back and forth, freezing, and thawing, and stifling, by turns. In about an hour, we stopped at another station; and as we left it Thompson came in with a bag, and said,—

'Cap., I'm a-going to chance him once more,—just this once; and if we don't fetch him this time, the thing for us to do, is to just throw up the sponge and withdraw from the canvass. That's the way I put it up.' He had brought a lot of chicken feathers, and dried apples, and leaf tobacco, and rags, and old shoes, and sulphur, and asafoetida, and one thing or another; and he, piled them on a breadth of sheet iron in the middle of the floor, and set fire to them.

When they got well started, I couldn't see, myself, how even the corpse could stand it. All that went before was just simply poetry to that smell,—but mind you, the original smell stood up out of it just as sublime as ever,—fact is, these other smells just seemed to give it a better hold; and my, how rich it was! I didn't make these reflections there—there wasn't time—made them on the platform. And breaking for the platform, Thompson got suffocated and fell; and before I got him dragged out, which I did by the collar, I was mighty near gone myself. When we revived, Thompson said dejectedly,—

'We got to stay out here, Cap. We got to do it. They ain't no other way. The Governor wants to travel alone, and he's fixed so he can outvote us.'

And presently he added,

'And don't you know, we're pisoned. It's our last trip, you can make up your mind to it. Typhoid fever is what's going to come of this. I feel it coming right now. Yes, sir, we're elected, just as sure as you're born.'

We were taken from the platform an hour later, frozen and insensible, at the next station, and I went straight off into a virulent fever, and never knew anything again for three weeks. I found out, then, that I had spent that awful night with a harmless box of rifles and a lot of innocent cheese; but the news was too late to save me; imagination had done its work, and my health was permanently shattered; neither Bermuda nor any other land can ever bring it back tome. This is my last trip; I am on my way home to die.

8

A TELEPHONIC CONVERSATION

Consider that a conversation by telephone—when you are simply sitting by and not taking any part in that conversation—is one of the solemnest curiosities of modern life. Yesterday, I was writing a deep article on a sublime philosophical subject while such a conversation was going on in the room. I noticed that one can always write best when somebody is talking through a telephone close by. Well, the thing began in this way. A member of our household came in and asked me to have our house put into communication with Mr. Bagley's downtown. I have observed, in many cities, that the sex always shrink from calling up the central office themselves. I don't know why, but they do. So I touched the bell, and this talk ensued:

CENTRAL OFFICE. gruffy. Hello!

I. Is it the Central Office?

C. O. Of course it is. What do you want?

I. Will you switch me on to the Bagleys, please?

C. O. All right. Just keep your ear to the telephone.

Then I heard k-look, k-look, k'look—klook-klook-klook-look-look! then a horrible 'gritting' of teeth, and finally a piping female voice: Y-e-s? rising inflection. Did you wish to speak to me?

Without answering, I handed the telephone to the applicant, and sat down. Then followed that queerest of all the queer things in this world— a conversation with only one end of it. You hear questions asked; you don't hear the answer. You hear invitations given; you hear no thanks in return. You have listening pauses of dead silence, followed by apparently irrelevant and unjustifiable exclamations of glad surprise or sorrow or dismay. You can't make head or tail of the talk, because you never hear anything that the person at the other end of the wire says. Well, I heard the following remarkable series of observations, all from the one tongue, and all shouted— for you can't ever persuade the sex to speak gently into a telephone:

Yes? Why, how did that happen?

Pause.

What did you say?

Pause.

Oh no, I don't think it was.

Pause.

No! Oh no, I didn't mean that. I meant, put it in while it is still boiling—or just before it comes to a boil.

Pause.

What?

Pause.

I turned it over with a backstitch on the selvage edge.

Pause.

Yes, I like that way, too; but I think it's better to baste it on with Valenciennes or bombazine, or something of that sort. It gives it such an air—and attracts so much noise.

Pause.

It's forty-ninth Deuteronomy, sixty-forth to ninety-seventh inclusive. I think we ought all to read it often.

Pause.

Perhaps so; I generally use a hair pin.

Pause.

What did you say? aside. Children, do be quiet!

Pause.

Oh! B flat! Dear me, I thought you said it was the cat!

Pause.

Since when?

Pause.

Why, I never heard of it.

Pause.

You astound me! It seems utterly impossible!

Pause.

Who did?

Pause.

Good-ness gracious!

Pause.

Well, what is this world coming to? Was it right in church?

Pause.

And was her mother there?

Pause.

Why, Mrs. Bagley, I should have died of humiliation! What did they do?

Long pause.

I can't be perfectly sure, because I haven't the notes by me; but I think it goes something like this: te-rolly-loll-loll, loll lolly-loll-loll, O tolly-loll-loll-lee-ly-li-I-do! And then repeat, you know.

Pause.

Yes, I think it is very sweet—and very solemn and impressive, if you get the andantino and the pianissimo right.

Pause.

Oh, gum-drops, gum-drops! But I never allow them to eat striped candy. And of course they can't, till they get their teeth, anyway.

Pause.

What?

Pause.

Oh, not in the least—go right on. He's here writing—it doesn't bother him.

Pause.

Very well, I'll come if I can. [Aside]. Dear me, how it does tire a person's arm to hold this thing up so long! I wish she'd—

Pause.

Oh no, not at all; I like to talk—but I'm afraid I'm keeping you from your affairs.

Pause.

Visitors?

Pause.

No, we never use butter on them.

Pause.

Yes, that is a very good way; but all the cook-books say they are very unhealthy when they are out of season. And he doesn't like them, anyway—especially canned.

Pause.

Oh, I think that is too high for them; we have never paid over fifty cents a bunch.

Pause.

Must you go? Well, good-bye.

Pause.

Yes, I think so. Good-bye.

Pause.

Four o'clock, then—I'll be ready. Good-bye.

Pause.

Thank you ever so much. Good-bye.

Pause.

Oh, not at all!—just as fresh—which? Oh, I'm glad to hear you say that. Good-bye.

Hangs up the telephone and says, 'Oh, it does tire a person's arm so!'

ITALIAN WITH GRAMMAR

I found that a person of large intelligence could read this beautiful language with considerable facility without a dictionary, but I presently found that to such a person a grammar could be of use at times. It is because, if he does not know the were's and the was's and the maybe's and the has-beens's apart, confusions and uncertainties can arise. He can get the idea that a thing is going to happen next week when the truth is that it has already happened week before last. Even more previously, sometimes. Examination and inquiry showed me that the adjectives and such things were frank and fair-minded and straightforward, and did not shuffle; it was the Verb that mixed the hands, it was the Verb that lacked stability, it was the Verb that had no permanent opinion about anything, it was the Verb that was always dodging the issue and putting out the light and making all the trouble.

Further examination, further inquiry, further reflection, confirmed this judgment, and established beyond peradventure the fact that the Verb was the storm-center. This discovery made plain the right and wise course to pursue in order to acquire certainty and exactness in understanding the statements which the newspaper was daily endeavoring to convey to me: I must catch a Verb and tame it. I must find out its ways, I must spot its eccentricities, I must penetrate its disguises, I must intelligently foresee and forecast at least the commoner of the dodges it was likely to try upon a stranger in given circumstances, I must get in on its main shifts and head them off, I must learn its game and play the limit.

I had noticed, in other foreign languages, that verbs are bred in families, and that the members of each family have certain features or resemblances that are common to that family and distinguish it from the other families—the other kin, the cousins and what not. I had noticed that this family-mark is not usually the nose or the hair, so to speak, but the tail—the Termination—and that these tails are quite definitely differentiated; in-so-much that an expert can tell a Pluperfect from a Subjunctive by its tail as easily and as certainly as a cowboy can tell a cow from a horse by the like process, the result of observation and culture. I should explain that I am speaking of legitimate verbs, those verbs which in the slang of the grammar are called Regular. There are other—I am not meaning to conceal this; others called Irregulars, born out of wedlock, of unknown and uninteresting parentage, and naturally destitute of family resemblances, as regards to all features, tails included. But of these pathetic outcasts I have nothing to say. I do not approve of them, I do not encourage them; I am prudishly delicate and sensitive, and I do not allow them to be used in my presence.

But, as I have said, I decided to catch one of the others and break it into harness. One is enough. Once familiar with its assortment of tails, you are immune; after that, no regular verb can conceal its specialty from you and make you think it is working the past or the future or the conditional or the unconditional when it is engaged in some other line of business—its tail will give it away. I found out all these things by myself, without a teacher.

I selected the verb amare, to love. Not for any personal reason, for I am indifferent about verbs; I care no more for one verb than for another, and have little or no respect for any of them; but in foreign languages you always begin with that one. Why, I don't know. It is merely habit, I suppose; the first teacher chose it, Adam was satisfied, and there hasn't been a successor since with originality enough to start a fresh one. For they are a pretty limited lot, you will admit that? Originality is not in their line; they can't think up anything new, anything to freshen up the old moss-grown dullness of the language lesson and put life and 'go' into it, and charm and grace and picturesqueness.

I knew I must look after those details myself; therefore, I thought them out and wrote them down, and set for the facchino and explained them to him, and said he must arrange a proper plant, and get together a good stock company among the contadini, and design the costumes, and distribute the parts; and drill the troupe, and be ready in three days to begin on this Verb in a shipshape and workman-like manner. I told him to put each grand division of it under a foreman, and each subdivision under a subordinate of the rank of sergeant or corporal or something like that, and to have a different uniform for each squad, so that I could tell a Pluperfect from a Compound Future without looking at the book; the whole battery to be under his own special and particular command, with the rank of Brigadier, and I to pay the freight.

I, then inquired into the character and possibilities of the selected verb, and was much disturbed to find that it was over my size, it being chambered for fifty-seven rounds—fifty-seven ways of saying I love without reloading; and yet none of them likely to convince a girl that was laying for a title, or a title that was laying for rocks.

It seemed to me that with my inexperience it would be foolish to go into action with this mitrailleuse, so I ordered it to the rear and told the facchino to provide something a little more primitive to start with, something less elaborate, some gentle old-fashioned flint-lock, smooth-bore, double-barreled thing, calculated to cripple at two hundred yards and kill at forty—an arrangement suitable for a beginner who could be satisfied with moderate results on the offstart and did not wish to take the whole territory in the first campaign.

But in vain. He was not able to mend the matter, all the verbs being of the same build, all Gatlings, all of the same caliber and delivery, fifty-seven to the volley, and fatal at a mile and a half. But he said the auxiliary verb avere, to have, was a tidy thing, and easy to handle in a seaway, and less likely to miss stays in going about than some of the others; so, upon his recommendation I chose that one, and told him to take it along and scrape its bottom and break out its spinnaker and get it ready for business.

I will explain that a facchino is a general-utility domestic. Mine was a horse-doctor in his better days, and a very good one.

At the end of three days, the facchino-doctor-brigadier was ready. I was also ready, with a stenographer. We were in a room called the Rope-Walk. This is a formidably long room, as is indicated by its facetious name, and is a good place for reviews. At 9:30 the F.-D.-B. took his place near me and gave the word of command; the drums began to rumble and thunder, the head of the forces appeared at an upper door, and the 'march-past' was on. Down they filed, a blaze of variegated color, each squad gaudy in a uniform of its own and bearing a banner inscribed with its verbal rank and quality: first the Present Tense in Mediterranean blue and old gold, then the Past Definite in scarlet and black, then the Imperfect in green and yellow, then the Indicative Future in the stars and stripes, then the Old Red Sandstone Subjunctive in purple and silver— and so on and so on, fifty-seven privates and twenty commissioned and non-commissioned officers; certainly one of the most fiery and dazzling and eloquent sights I have ever beheld. I could not keep back the tears. Presently:

'Halt!' commanded the Brigadier.

'Front—face!'

'Right dress!'

'Stand at ease!'

'One—two—three. In unison—recite!'

It was fine. In one noble volume of sound of all the fifty-seven Haves in the Italian language burst forth in an exalting and splendid confusion. Then came commands:

'About—face! Eyes—front! Helm alee—hard aport! Forward—march!' and the drums let go again.

When the last Termination had disappeared, the commander said the instruction drill would now begin, and asked for suggestions. I said:

'They say I have, thou hast, he has, and so on, but they don't say what. It will be better, and more definite, if they have something to have; just an object, you know, a something—anything will do; anything that will give the listener a sort of personal as well as grammatical interest in their joys and complaints, you see.'

He said:

'It is a good point. Would a dog do?'

I said I did not know, but we could try a dog and see. So he sent out an aide-de-camp to give the order to add the dog.

The six privates of the Present Tense now filed in, in charge of Sergeant Avere (to have), and displaying their banner. They formed in line of battle, and recited, one at a time, thus:

'Io ho un cane, I have a dog.'

'Tu hai un cane, thou hast a dog.'

'Egli ha un cane, he has a dog.'

'Noi abbiamo un cane, we have a dog.'

'Voi avete un cane, you have a dog.'

'Eglino hanno un cane, they have a dog.'

No comment followed. They returned to camp, and I reflected a while. The commander said:

'I fear you are disappointed.'

'Yes,' I said; 'they are too monotonous, too singsong, to dead-and-alive; they have no expression, no elocution. It isn't natural; it could never happen in real life. A person who had just acquired a dog is either blame' glad or blame' sorry. He is not on the fence. I never saw a case. What the nation do you suppose is the matter with these people?'

He thought maybe the trouble was with the dog. He said:

'These are contadini, you know, and they have a prejudice against dogs— that is, against marimane. Marimana dogs stand guard over people's vines and olives, you know, and are very savage, and thereby a grief and an inconvenience to persons who want other people's things at night. In my judgment they have taken this dog for a marimana, and have soured on him.'

I saw that the dog was a mistake, and not functionable: we must try something else; something, if possible, that could evoke sentiment, interest, feeling.

'What is cat, in Italian?' I asked.

'Gatto.'

'Is it a gentleman cat, or a lady?'

'Gentleman cat.'

'How are these people as regards that animal?'

'We-ll, they—they—'

'You hesitate: that is enough. How are they about chickens?'

He tilted his eyes toward heaven in mute ecstasy. I understood.

'What is chicken, in Italian?' I asked.

'Pollo, Podere.' (Podere is Italian for master. It is a title of courtesy, and conveys reverence and admiration.) 'Pollo is one chicken by itself; when there are enough present to constitute a plural, it is polli.'

'Very well, polli will do. Which squad is detailed for duty next?'

'The Past Definite.'

'Send out and order it to the front—with chickens. And let them understand that we don't want any more of this cold indifference.'

He gave the order to an aide, adding, with a haunting

tenderness in his tone and a watering mouth in his aspect:

'Convey to them the conception that these are unprotected chickens.' He turned to me, saluting with his hand to his temple, and explained, 'It will inflame their interest in the poultry, sire.'

A few minutes elapsed. Then the squad marched in and formed up, their faces glowing with enthusiasm, and the file-leader shouted:

'Ebbi polli, I had chickens!'

'Good!' I said. 'Go on, the next.'

'Avest polli, thou hadst chickens!'

'Fine! Next!'

'Ebbe polli, he had chickens!'

'Moltimoltissimo! Go on, the next!'

'Avemmo polli, we had chickens!'

'Basta-basta aspettatto avanti—last man—charge!'

'Ebbero polli, they had chickens!'

Then they formed in echelon, by columns of fours, refused the left, and retired in great style on the double-quick. I was enchanted, and said:

'Now, doctor, that is something like! Chickens are the ticket, there is no doubt about it. What is the next squad?'

'The Imperfect.'

'How does it go?'

'Io avena, I had, tu avevi, thou hadst, egli avena, he had, noi av—'

Wait—we've just had the hads. what are you giving me?'

'But this is another breed.'

'What do we want of another breed? Isn't one breed enough? Had is had, and your tricking it out in a fresh way of spelling isn't going to make it any hadder than it was before; now you know that yourself.'

'But there is a distinction—they are not just the same Hads.'

'How do you make it out?'

'Well, you use that first Had when you are referring to something that happened at a named and sharp and perfectly definite moment; you use the other when the thing happened at a vaguely defined time and in a more prolonged and indefinitely continuous way.'

'Why, doctor, it is pure nonsense; you know it yourself. Look here: If I have had a had, or have wanted to have had a had, or was in a position right then and there to have had a had that hadn't had any chance to go out hadding on account of this foolish discrimination which lets one Had go hadding in any kind of indefinite grammatical weather but restricts the other one to definite and datable meteoric convulsions, and keeps it pining around and watching the barometer all the time, and liable to get sick through confinement and lack of exercise, and all that sort of thing, why—why, the inhumanity of it is enough, let alone the wanton superfluity and uselessness of any such a loafing consumptive hospital-bird of a Had taking up room and cumbering the place for nothing. These finical refinements revolt me; it is not right, it is not honorable; it is constructive nepotism to keep in office a Had that is so delicate it can't come out when the wind's in the nor'west—I won't have this dude on the payroll. Cancel his exequatur; and look here—'

'But you miss the point. It is like this. You see—'

'Never mind explaining, I don't care anything about it. Six Hads is enough for me; anybody that needs twelve, let him subscribe; I don't want any stock in a Had Trust. Knock out the Prolonged and Indefinitely Continuous; four-fifths of it is water, anyway.'

'But I beg you, podere! It is often quite indispensable in cases where—'

'Pipe the next squad to the assault!'

But it was not to be; for at that moment the dull boom of the noon gun floated up out of far-off Florence, followed by the usual softened jangle of church-bells, Florentine and suburban, that bursts out in murmurous response; by labor-union law the Colazione [1] must stop; stop promptly, stop instantly, stop definitely, like the chosen and best of the breed of Hads.

1. Colazione is Italian for a collection, a meeting, a seance, a sitting.—M.T.

10

THE PRIVATE HISTORY OF
A CAMPAIGN THAT FAILED

You have heard from a great many people who did something in the war, is it not fair and right that you listen a little moment to one who started out to do something in it but didn't? Thousands entered the war, got just a taste of it, and then stepped out again permanently. These, by their very numbers, are respectable and therefore entitled to a sort of voice, not a loud one, but a modest one, not a boastful one but an apologetic one. They ought not be allowed much space among better people, people who did something. I grant that, but they ought at least be allowed to state why they didn't do anything and also to explain the process by which they didn't do anything. Surely this kind of light must have some sort of value.

Out west there was a good deal of confusion in men's minds during the first months of the great trouble, a good deal of unsettledness, of leaning first this way, then that, and then the other way. It was hard for us to get our bearings. I call to mind an example of this. I was piloting on the Mississippi when the news came that South Carolina had gone out of the Union on the 20th of December, 1860. My pilot mate was a New Yorker. He was strong for the Union; so was I. But he would not listen to me with any patience, my loyalty was smirched, to his eye, because my father had owned slaves. I said in palliation of this dark fact that I had heard my father say, some years before he died, that slavery was a great wrong and he would free the solitary Negro he then owned if he could think it right to give away the property of the family when he was so straitened in means. My mate retorted that a mere impulse was nothing, anyone could pretend to a good impulse, and went on decrying my Unionism and libelling my ancestry. A month later, the secession atmosphere had considerably thickened on the Lower Mississippi and I became a rebel; so did he. We were together in New Orleans the 26th of January, when Louisiana went out of the Union. He did his fair share of the rebel shouting but was opposed to letting me do mine. He said I came of bad stock, of a father who had been willing to set slaves free. In the following summer, he was piloting a Union gunboat and shouting for the Union again and I was in the Confederate army. I held his note for some borrowed money. He was one of the most upright men I ever knew but he repudiated that note without hesitation because I was a rebel and the son of a man who owned slaves.

In that summer of 1861, the first wash of the wave of war broke upon the shores of Missouri. Our state was invaded by the Union forces. They took possession of St. Louis, Jefferson Barracks, and some other points. The governor, Calib Jackson, issued his proclamation calling out fifty thousand militia to repel the invader.

I was visiting in the small town where my boyhood had been spent, Hannibal, Marion County. Several of us got together in a secret place by night and formed ourselves into a military company. One Tom Lyman, a young fellow of a good deal of spirit but of no military experience, was made captain; I was made second lieutenant. We had no first lieutenant, I do not know why, it was so long ago. There were fifteen of us. By the advice of an innocent connected with the organization we called ourselves the Marion Rangers. I do not remember that anyone found fault with the name. I did not, I thought it sounded quite well. The young fellow who proposed this title was perhaps a fair sample of the kind of stuff we were made of. He was young, ignorant, good natured, well meaning, trivial, full of romance, and given to reading chivalric novels and singing forlorn love ditties. He had some pathetic little nickel plated aristocratic instincts and detested his name, which was Dunlap, detested it partly because it was nearly as common in that region as Smith but mainly because it had a plebian sound to his ears. So he tried to ennoble it by writing it in this way; d'Unlap. That contented his eye but left his ear unsatisfied, for people gave the new name the same old pronunciation, emphasis on the front end of it. He then did the bravest thing that can be imagined, a thing to make one shiver when one remembers how the world is given to resenting shams and affectations, he began to write his name so; d'Un'Lap. And he waited patiently through the long storm of mud that was flung at his work of art and he had his reward at last, for he lived to see that name accepted and the emphasis put where he wanted it put by people who had known him all his life, and to whom the tribe of Dunlaps had been as familiar as the rain and the sunshine for forty years. So sure of victory at last is the courage that can wait. He said he had found by consulting some ancient French chronicles that the name was rightly and originally written d'Un'Lap and said that if it were translated into English it would mean Peterson, Lap, Latin or Greek, he said, for stone or rock, same as the French pierre, that is to say, Peter, d' of or from, un, a or one, hence d'Un'Lap, of or from a stone or a Peter, that is to say, one who is the son of a stone, the son of a peter, Peterson. Our militia company were not learned and the explanation confused them, so they called him Peterson Dunlap. He proved useful to us in his way, he named our camps for us and generally struck a name that was 'no slouch' as the boys said.

That is one sample of us. Another was Ed Stevens, son of

the town jeweller, trim built, handsome, graceful, neat as a cat, bright, educated, but given over entirely to fun. There was nothing serious in life to him. As far as he was concerned, this military expedition of ours was simply a holiday. I should say about half of us looked upon it in much the same way, not consciously perhaps, but unconsciously. We did not think, we were not capable of it. As for myself, I was full of unreasoning joy to be done with turning out of bed at midnight and four in the morning, for a while grateful to have a change, new scenes, new occupations, a new interest. In my thoughts that was as far as I went. I did not go into the details, as a rule, one doesn't at twenty four.

Another sample was Smith, the blacksmith's apprentice. This vast donkey had some pluck, of a slow and sluggish nature, but a soft heart. At one time, he would knock a horse down from some impropriety and at another he would get homesick and cry. However, he had one ultimate credit to his account which some of us hadn't. He stuck to the war and was killed in battle at last.

Joe Bowers, another sample, was a huge, good natured, flax headed lubber, lazy, sentimental, full of harmless brag, a grumbler by nature, an experience and industrious ambitious and often quite picturesque liar, and yet not a successful one for he had no intelligent training but was allowed to come up just anyways. This life was serious enough to him, and seldom satisfactory. But he was a good fellow anyway and the boys all liked him. He was made orderly sergeant, Stevens was made corporal.

These samples will answer and they are quite fair ones. Well, this herd of cattle started for the war. What could you expect of them? They did as well as they knew how, but really, what was justly expected of them? Nothing I should say. And that is what they did.

We waited for a dark night, for caution and secrecy were necessary, then toward midnight we stole in couples and from various directions to the Griggith place beyond town. From that place we set out together on foot. Hannibal lies at the extreme south eastern corner of Marion County, on the Mississippi river. Our objective point was the hamlet of New London, ten miles away in Ralls County.

The first hour was all fun, all idle nonsense and laughter. But that could not be kept up. The steady drudging became like work, the play had somehow oozed out of it, the stillness of the woods and the sombreness of the night began to throw a depressing influence over the spirits of the boys and presently the talking died out and each person shut himself up in his own thoughts. During the last half of the second hour, nobody said a word.

Now we approached a log farmhouse where, according to reports, there was a guard of five Union soldiers. Lyman called a halt, and there, in the deep gloom of the overhanging branches, he began to whisper a plan of assault upon the house, which made the gloom more depressing than it was before. We realized with a cold suddenness that here was no jest—we were standing face to face with actual war. We were equal to the occasion. In our response there was no hesitation, no indecision. We said that if Lyman wanted to meddle with those soldiers he could go ahead and do it, but if he waited for us to follow him he would wait a long time.

Lyman urged, pleaded, tried to shame us into it, but it had no effect. Our course was plain in our minds, our minds were made up. We would flank the farmhouse, go out around. And that was what we did.

We struck into the woods and entered upon a rough time, stumbling over roots, getting tangled in vines and torn by briers. At last we reached an open place in a safe region and we sat down, blown and hot, to cool off and nurse our scratches and bruises. Lyman was annoyed but the rest of us were cheerful. We had flanked the farmhouse. We had made our first military movement and it was a success. We had nothing to fret about, we were feeling just the other way. Horse play and laughing began again. The expedition had become a holiday frolic once more.

Then we had two more hours of dull trudging and ultimate silence and depression. Then about dawn, we straggled into New London, soiled, heel blistered, fagged with out little march, and all of us, except Stevens, in a sour and raspy humour and privately down on the war. We stacked our shabby old shotguns in Colonel Ralls's barn and then went in a body and breakfasted with that veteran of the mexican war. Afterward, he took us to a distant meadow, and there, in the shade of a tree, we listened to an old fashioned speech from him, full of gunpowder and glory, full of that adjective piling, mixed metaphor and windy declamation which was regraded as eloquence in that ancient time and region and then he swore on a bible to be faithful to the State of Missouri and drive all invaders from her soil no matter whence they may come or under what flag they might march. This mixed us considerably and we could not just make out what service we were involved in, but Colonel Ralls, the practised politician and phrase juggler, was not similarly in doubt. He knew quite clearly he had invested us in the cause of the Southern Confederacy. He closed the solemnities by belting around me the sword which his neighbour, Colonel brown, had worn at Beuna Vista and Molino del Ray and he accompanied this act with another impressive blast.

Then we formed in line of battle and marched four hours to a shady and pleasant piece of woods on the border of a far reaching expanse of a flowery prairie. It was an enchanting region for war, our kind of war.

We pierced the forest about half a mile and took up a strong position with some low and rocky hills behind us, and a purling limpid creek in front. Straightaway half the command was in swimming and the other half fishing. The ass with the french name gave the position a romantic title but it was too long so the boys shortened and simplified it to Camp Ralls.

We occupied an old maple sugar camp whose half rotted troughs were still propped against the trees. A long corn crib served from sleeping quarters from the battalion. On our left, half a mile away, were Mason's farm and house, and he was a friend to the cause. Shortly after noon, the farmers began to arrive from several different directions with mules and horses for our use, and these they lent us for as long as the war might last, which, they judged, might be about three months. The animals were of all sizes all colours and all breeds. They were mainly young and frisky and nobody in the command could stay on them long at a time, for we were town boys and ignorant of horsemanship. The creature that fell to my share was a very small mule, and yet so quick and active he could throw me off without difficulty and it did this whenever I got on. Then it would bray, stretching its neck out, laying its ears back and spreading its jaws till you could see down to its works. If I took it by the bridle and tried to lead it off the grounds it would sit down and brace back and no one could ever budge it. However, I was not entirely destitute of military resources and I did presently manage to spoil this game, for I had seen many a steamboat aground in my time and knew a trick or two which even a grounded mule would be obliged to respect. There was a well by the corn crib so I substituted thirty fathom of rope for the bridle and fetched him home with the windlass.

I will anticipate here sufficiently to say that we did learn to ride after some days' practice, but never well. We could not learn to like our animals. They were not choice ones and most of them had annoying peculiarities of one kind or another. Stevens's horse would carry him, when he was not noticing, under the huge excrescences which for on the trunks of oak trees and wipe him out of the saddle this way. Stevens got several bad hurts. Sergeant Bowers's horse was very large and tall, slim with long legs, and looked like a railroad bridge. His size enabled him to reach all about, and as far as he wanted to go, so he was always biting

Bowers's legs. On the march, in the sun, Bowers slept a good deal and as soon as the horse recognized he was asleep he would reach around and bite him on the leg. His legs were black and blue with bites. This was the only thing that could make him swear, but this always did, whenever his horse bit him he swore, and of course, Stevens, who laughed at everything, laughed at this and would get into such convulsions over it as to lose his balance and fall off his horse, and then Bowers, already irritated by the pain of the horse bite, would resent the laughter with hard language, and there would be a quarrel so that horse made no end of trouble and bad blood in the command.

However, I will get back to where I was, our first afternoon in the sugar camp. The sugar troughs came very handy as horse troughs and we had plenty of corn to fill them with. I ordered Sergeant Bowers to feed my mule, but he said that if I reckoned he went to war to be a dry nurse to a mule it wouldn't take me very long to find out my mistake. I believed that this was insubordination but I was full of uncertainties about everything military so I let the matter pass and went and ordered Smith, the blacksmith's apprentice, to feed the mule, but he merely gave me a large, cold, sarcastic grin, such as an ostensibly seven year old horse gives you when you lift up his lip and find he is fourteen, and turned his back on me. I then went to the captain and asked if it were not right and proper and military for me to have an orderly. He said it was, but as there was only one orderly in the corps, it was but right he himself should have Bowers on his staff. Bowers said he wouldn't serve on anyone's staff and if anybody thought he could make him, let him try. So, of course, the matter had to be dropped, there was no other way.

Next, nobody would cook. It was considered a degradation so we had no dinner. We lazed the rest of the pleasant afternoon away, some dozing under trees, some smoking cob pipes and talking sweethearts and war, others playing games. By late supper time, all hands were famished and to meet the difficulty, all hands turned to on an equal footing, and gathered wood, built fires, and cooked the evening meal. Afterward, everything was smooth for a while then trouble broke out between the corporal and the sergeant, each claiming to rank the other. Nobody knew which was the higher office so Lyman had to settle the matter by making the rank of both officers equal. The commander of an ignorant crew like that has many troubles and vexations which probably do not occur in the regular army at all. However, with the song singing and yarn spinning around the campfire everything presently became serene again, and by and by we raked the corn down one level in one end of the crib and all went to bed on it, tying a horse to the door so he would neigh if anyone tried to get in. (it was always my impression that was always what the horse was there for and I know it was the impression of at least one other of the command, for we talked about it at the time and admired the military ingenuity of the device, but when I was out west three years ago, I was told by Mr. A. G. Fuqua, a member of our company, that the horse was his, that the tying him at the door was a mere matter of forgetfulness and that to attribute it to intelligent invention was to give him quite too much credit. In support of his position, he called my attention to the suggestive fact that the artifice was not employed again. I had not thought of that before.)

We had some horsemanship drill every forenoon, then, afternoons, we rode off here and there in squads a few miles and visited the farmer's girls and had a youthful good time and got an honest dinner or supper, and then home again to camp, happy and content.

For a time, life was idly delicious. It was perfect. There was no war to mar it. Then came some farmers with an alarm one day. They said it was rumoured that the enemy were advancing in our direction from over Hyde's prairie. The result was a sharp stir among us and general consternation. It was a rude awakening from out pleasant trance. The rumour was but a rumour, nothing definite about it, so in the confusion we did not know which way to retreat. Lyman was not for retreating at all in these uncertain circumstances but he found that if he tried to maintain that attitude he would fare badly, for the command were in no humour to put up with insubordination. So, he yielded the point and called a council of war, to consist of himself and three other officers, but the privates made such a fuss about being left out we had to allow them to remain, for they were already present and doing most of the talking too. The question was, which way to retreat; but all were so flurried that nobody even seemed to have even a guess to offer. Except Lyman. He explained in a few calm words, that inasmuch as the enemy were approaching from over Hyde's prairie our course was simple. All we had to do was not retreat toward him, another direction would suit our purposes perfectly. Everybody saw in a moment how true this was and how wise, so Lyman got a great many compliments. It was now decided that we should fall back on Mason's farm.

It was after dark by this time and as we could not know how soon the enemy might arrive, it did not seem best to try to take the horses and things with us, so we only took the guns and ammunition, and started at once. The route was very rough and hilly and rocky, and presently the night grew very black and rain began to fall, so we had a troublesome time of it, struggling and stumbling along in the dark and soon some person slipped and fell, and then the next person behind stumbled over him and fell, and so did the rest, one after the other, and then Bowers came along with the keg of powder in his arms, while the command were all mixed together, arms and legs on the muddy slope, and so he fell, of course, with the keg and this started the whole detachment down the hill in a body and they landed in a brook at the bottom in a pile and each that was undermost was pulling the hair, scratching and biting those that were on top of him and those that were being scratched and bitten scratching and biting the rest in their turn, and all saying they would die before they would ever go to war again if they ever got out of this brook this time and the invader might rot for all they cared, and the country along with him, and all such talk as that which was dismal to hear and take part in, in such smothered, low voices, and such a grisly dark place and so wet, and the enemy, maybe, coming along at any moment.

The keg of powder was lost, and the guns too; so the growling and complaining continued straight along while the brigade pawed around the pasty hill side and slopped around in the brook hunting for these things; consequently, we lost considerable time at this, and then we heard a sound and held our breath and listened, and it seemed to be the enemy coming, though it could have been a cow, for it had a cough like a cow, but we did not wait but left a couple of guns behind and struck out for Mason's again as briskly as we could scramble along in the dark. But we got lost, presently in among the rugged little ravines and wasted a deal of time finding the way again so it was after nine when we reached Mason's stile at last; and then before we could open our mouths to give the countersign several dogs came bounding over the fence with a great riot and noise, and each of them took a soldier by the slack of his trousers and began to back away with him. We could not shoot the dogs without endangering the persons they were attached to so we had to look on helpless at what was perhaps the most mortifying spectacle of the Civil War. There was light enough and to spare, for the Mason's had now run out on the porch with candles in tier hands. The old man and his son came and undid the dogs without difficulty, all but Bowers's; but they couldn't undo his dog, they didn't know his combination, he was of the bull kind and seemed to be set with a Yale time-lock, but they got him loose at last with some scalding water, of which Boweres got his share and returned thanks. Peterson Dunlap, afterwards made up a fine name for this engagement and also for the night march which preceded it but both have long ago faded out of my memory.

We now went into the house and they began to ask us a world of questions, whereby it presently came out that we did not know anything concerning who or what we were running from; so the old gentleman made himself very frank and said we were a curious breed of soldiers and guessed we could be depended on to end up the war in time, because the no governor could afford the expense of the shoe leather we should cost it trying to follow us around.

'Marion Rangers! Good name, b'gosh,' said he. And wanted to why we hadn't had a picket guard at the place where the road entered the prairie, and why we hadn't sent out a scouting party to spy out the enemy and bring us an account of his strength, and so on, before jumping up and stampeding out of a strong position upon a mere vague rumour, and so on and so forth, till he made us all feel shabbier than the dogs had done, not so half enthusiastically welcome. So we went to bed shamed and low spirited, except Stevens. Soon Stevens began to devise a garment for Bowers which could be made to automatically display his battle scars to the grateful or conceal them from the envious, according to his occasions, but Bowers was in no humour for this, so there was a fight and when it was over Stevens had some battle scars of his own to think about.

Then we got a little sleep. But after all we had gone through, our activities were not over for the night, for about two o'clock in the morning we heard a shout of warning from down the lane, accompanied by a chorus from all the dogs, and in a moment everybody was up and flying around to find out what the alarm was about. The alarmist was a horseman who gave notice that a detachment of Union soldiers was on its way from Hannibal with orders to capture and hang any bands like our which it could find. Farmer Mason was in a flurry this time himself. He hurried us out of the house with all haste, and sent one of his negroes with us to show us where to hide ourselves and our telltale guns among the ravines half a mile away,. It was raining heavily.

We struck down the lane, then across some rocky pasture land which offered good advantages fro stumbling; consequently we were down in the mud most of the time, and every time a man went down he black guarded the war and everybody connected with it, and gave himself the master dose of all for being so foolish as to go into it. At last, we reached the wooded mouth of a ravine, and there we huddled ourselves under the streaming trees and sent the negro back home. It was a dismal and heart breaking time. We were like to be drowned with the rain, deafened with the howling wind and the booming thunder, and blinded by the lightning. It was indeed a wild night. The drenching we were getting was misery enough, but a deeper misery still was the reflection that the halter might end us before we were a day older. A death of this shameful sort had not occurred to us as being among the possibilities of war. It took the romance all out of the campaign and turned our dreams of glory into a repulsive nightmare. As for doubting that so barbarous an order had been given, not one of us did that.

The long night wore itself out at last, and then the Negro came to us with the news that the alarm had manifestly been a false one and that breakfast would soon be ready. Straightaway we were light-hearted again and the world was bright and full of life, as full of hope and promise as ever; for we were young then. How long ago that was! Twenty four years.

The mongrel child of philology named the night's refuge Camp Devastation and no soul objected. The Masons gave us a Missouri country breakfast in Missourian abundance, and we needed it. Hot biscuits, hot wheat bread, prettily crossed in a lattice pattern on top, hot corn pone, fried chicken, bacon, coffee, eggs, milk, buttermilk etc. and the world may be confidently challenged to furnish the equal of such a breakfast, as it is cooked in the South.

We stayed several days at Mason's and after all these years the memory of the stillness and dullness and lifelessness of that slumberous farmhouse still oppresses my spirit as with a sense of the presence of death and mourning. There was nothing to do. Nothing to think about. There was no interest in life. The male part of the household were away in the fields all day, the women were busy and out of our sight, There was no sound but the plaintive wailing of a spinning wheel forever moaning out from some distant room, the most lonesome sound in nature, a sound steeped and sodden with homesickness and the emptiness of life. The family went to bed about dark every night and as we were not invited to intrude any new customs we naturally followed theirs. Those nights were a hundred years long to youths accustomed to being up till twelve. We lay awake and miserable till that hour ovariotomy and grew old and decrepit waiting through the still eternities for the clock strikes. This was no place for town boys. So at last, it was with something very like joy that we received word that the enemy were on out track again. With a new birth of the old warrior spirit, we sprang to our places in line of battle and fell back on Camp Ralls.

Captain Lyman had taken a hint from Mason's talk, and he now gave orders that our camp should be guarded from surprise by the posting of pickets. I was ordered to place a picket at the forks of the road in Hyde's prairie. Night shut down black and threatening. I told Sergeant Bowers to out to that place and stay till midnight, and, just as I was expecting, he said he wouldn't do it. I tried to get others to go but all refused. Some excused themselves on account of the weather, but the rest were frank enough to say they wouldn't go in any kind of weather. This kind of thing sounds odd now, and impossible, but there was no surprise in it at the time. On the contrary, it seemed a perfectly natural thing to do. There were scores of little camps scattered over missouri where the same thing was happening. These camps were composed of young men who had been born and reared to a sturdy independence and who did not know what it meant to be ordered around by Tom, Dick, and Harry, who they had known familiarly all their lives in the village or the farm. It is quite within the probabilities that this same thing was happening all over the South. James Redpath recognized the justice of this assumption and furnished the following instance in support of it. During a short stay in East Tennessee, he was in a citizen colonel's tent one day talking, when a big private appeared at the door and, without salute or other circumlocution, said to the colonel;

'Say, Jim, I'm goin' home for a few days.'

'What for?'

'Well, I hain't b'en there for a right smart while and I'd like to see how things is comin' on.'

'How long are you gonna be gone?'

'Bout two weeks.'

'Well, don't be gone longer than that and get back sooner if you can.'

That was all, and the citizen officer resumed his conversation where the private had broken it off. This was in the first months of the war of course. The camps in our part of Missouri were under Brigadier-General Thomas H. Harris. He was a townsman of ours, a first rate fellow and well liked, but we had all familiarly known him as the soles and modest-salaried operator in the telegraph office, where he had to send about one despatch a week in ordinary times and two when there was a rush of business. Consequently, when he appeared in our midst one day on the wing, and delivered a military command of some sort in a large military fashion, nobody was surprised at the response which he got from the assembled soldiery.

'Oh, now what'll you take to don't, Tom Harris?'

It was quite the natural thing. One might justly imagine that we were hopeless material for the war. And so we seemed in our ignorant state, but there were those among us who afterward learned the grim trade, learned to obey like machines, became valuable soldiers, fought all through the war, and came out at the end with excellent records. One of the very boys who refused to go out on picket duty that night and called me an ass for thinking he would expose himself to danger in such a foolhardy way, had become distinguished for intrepidity before he was a year older.

I did secure my picket that might, not by authority but by diplomacy. I got Bowers to go by agreeing to exchange ranks with him for the time being and go along and stand the watch with him as his subordinate. We stayed out there a couple of dreary hours in the pitchy darkness and the rain, with nothing to modify the dreariness but Bower's monotonous growling at the war and the weather, then we began to nod and presently found it next to impossible to stay in the saddle, so we gave up the tedious job and went back to the camp without interruption or objection from anybody and the enemy could have done the same, for there were no sentries. Everybody was asleep, at midnight there was nobody to send out another picket so none was sent. We never tried to establish a watch at night again, as far as I remember, but we generally kept a picket out in the daytime.

In that camp the whole command slept on the corn in the big corn crib and there was usually a general row before morning, for the place was full of rats and they would scramble over the boys' bodies and faces, annoying and irritating everybody, and now and then they would bite someone's toe, and the person who owned the toe would start up and magnify his english and begin to throw corn in the dark. The ears were half as heavy as bricks and when they struck they hurt. The persons struck would respond and inside of five minutes everyman would be locked in a death grip with his neighbour. There was a grievous deal of blood shed in the corn crib but this was all that was spilt while I was in the war. No, that is not quite true. But for one circumstance it would have been all.

Our scares were frequent. Every few days rumours would come that the enemy were approaching. In these cases we always fell back on some other camp of ours; we never stayed where we were. But the rumours always turned out to be false, so at last we even began to grow indifferent to them. One night a negro was sent to our corn crib with the same old warning, the enemy was hovering in our neighbourhood. We all said let him hover. We resolved to stay still and be comfortable. It was a fine warlike resolution, and no doubt we all felt the stir of it in our veins—for a moment. We had been having a very jolly time, that was full of horseplay and schoolboy hilarity, but that cooled down and presently the fast waning fire of forced jokes and forced laughs died out altogether and the company became silent. Silent and nervous. And soon uneasy—worried and apprehensive. We had said we would stay and we were committed. We could have been persuaded to go but there was nobody brave enough to suggest it. An almost noiseless movement began in the dark by a general but unvoiced impulse. When the movement was completed, each man knew that he was not the only person who had crept to the front wall and had his eye at a crack between the logs. No, we were all there, all there with our hearts in our throats and staring out towards the sugar-troughs where the forest footpath came through. It was late and there was a deep woodsy stillness everywhere. There was a veiled moonlight which was only just strong enough to enable us to mark the general shapes of objects. Presently, a muffled sound caught our ears and we recognized the hoof-beats of a horse or horses. And right away, a figure appeared in the forest path; it could have been made of smoke, its mass had such little sharpness of outline. It was a man on horseback, and it seemed to me that there were others behind him. I got a hold of a gun in the dark, and pushed it through a crack between the logs, hardly knowing what I was doing, I was so dazed with fright. Somebody said 'Fire!' I pulled the trigger, I seemed to see a hundred flashes and a hundred reports, then I saw the man fall down out of the saddle. My first feeling was of surprised gratification; my first impulse was an apprentice-sportsman's impulse to run and pick up his game. Somebody said, hardly audibly, 'Good, we've got him. Wait for the rest!' But the rest did not come. There was not a sound, not the whisper of a leaf; just the perfect stillness, an uncanny kind of stillness which was all the more uncanny on account of the damp, earthy, late night smells now rising and pervading it. Then, wondering, we crept out stealthily and approached the man. When we got to him, the moon revealed him distinctly. He was laying on his back with his arms abroad, his mouth was open and his chest was heaving with long gasps, and his white shirt front was splashed with blood. The thought shot through me that I was a murderer, that I had killed a man, a man who had never done me any harm. That was the coldest sensation that ever went through my marrow. I was down by him in a moment, helplessly stroking his forehead, and I would have given anything then, my own life freely, to make him again what he had been five minutes before. And all the boys seemed to be feeling the same way; they hung over him, full of pitying interest, and tried all they could to help him, and said all sorts of regretful things. They had forgotten all about the enemy, they thought only of this one forlorn unit of the foe. Once my imagination persuaded me that the dying man gave me a reproachful look out of the shadow of his eyes, and it seemed to me that I could rather that he had stabbed me than he had done that. He muttered and mumbled like a dreamer in his sleep about his wife and his child, and, I thought with a new despair, 'This thing that I have done does not end with him; it falls upon them too, and they never did me any harm, any more than he.'

In a little while, the man was dead. He was killed in war, killed in fair and legitimate war, killed in battles as you may say, and yet he was as sincerely mourned by the opposing force as if he had been their brother. The boys stood there a half-hour sorrowing over him and recalling the details of the tragedy, and wondering who he might be and if he was a spy, and saying if they had it to do over again, they would not hurt him unless he attacked them first. It soon turned out that mine was not the only shot fired; there were five others, a division of the guilt which was a great relief to me since it in some degree lightened and diminished the burden I was carrying. There were six shots fired at once but I was not in my right mind at the time, and my heated imagination had magnified my one shot into a volley.

The man was not in uniform and was not armed. He was a stranger in the country, that was all we ever found out about him. The thought of he got to preying on me every night, I could not get rid of it. I could not drive it away, the taking of that unoffending life seemed such a wanton thing. And it seemed an epitome of war, that all war must just be the killing of strangers against whom you feel no personal animosity, strangers who in other circumstances you would help if you found them in trouble, and who would help you if you needed it. My campaign was spoiled. It seemed to me that I was not rightly equipped for this awful business, that war was intended for men and I for a child's nurse. I resolved to retire from this avocation of sham soldier-ship while I could retain some remanent of my self-respect. These morbid thoughts clung to me against reason, for at the bottom I did not believe I had touched this man. The law of probabilities decreed me guiltless of his blood for in all my small experiences with guns, I had not hit anything I had tried to hit, and I knew I had done my best to hit him. Yet there was no solace in the thought. Against a diseased imagination, demonstration goes for nothing.

The rest of my war experience was of a piece with what I have already told of it. We kept monotonously falling back upon one camp or another and eating up the farmers and their families. They ought to have shot us; on the contrary they were as hospitably kind and courteous to us as if we had deserved it.

In one of these camps we found Ab Grimes, an upper Mississippi pilot who afterwards became famous as a daredevil rebel spy, whose career bristled with desperate adventures. The loom and style of his comrades suggested that they had not come into the war to play and their deeds made good the conjecture later. They were fine horsemen and good revolver shots, but their favourite arm was the lasso. Each had one at his pommel, and could snatch a man out of his saddle with it ovariotomy, on a full gallop, at any reasonable distance.

In another camp, the chief was a fierce and profane old black-smith of sixty and he had furnished his twenty recruits with gigantic, home-made bowie-knives, to be swung with two hands like the machetes of the Isthmus. It was a grisly spectacle to see that earnest band practising their murderous cuts and slashes under the eye of that remorseless old fanatic.

The last camp which we fell back on was in a hollow near the village of Florida where I was born, in Monroe County. Here we were warned one day that a Union Colonel was sweeping down on us with a whole regiment at his heels. This looked decidedly serious. Our boys went apart and consulted; then we went back and told the other companies present that the war was a disappointment to us and we were going to disband. They were getting ready themselves to fall back on some place or another, and we were only waiting for General Tom Harris, who was expected to arrive at any moment, so they tried to persuade us to wait a little while but the majority of us said no, we were accustomed to falling back and didn't need any of Harris's help, we could get along perfectly without him and save time too. So, about half of our fifteen men, including myself, mounted, and left on the instant; the others yielded to persuasion, and stayed—stayed through the war.

An hour later we met General Harris on the road, with two or three people in his company, his staff probably, but we could not tell; none of them were in uniform; uniforms had not come into vogue among us yet. Harris ordered us back, but we told him there was a Union colonel coming with a whole regiment in his wake and it looked as if there was going to be a disturbance, so we had concluded to go home. He raged a little bit, but it was of no use, our minds were made up. We had done our share, killed one man, exterminated one army, such as it was; let him go and kill the rest and that would end the war. I did not see that brisk young general again until last year; he was wearing white hair and whiskers.

In time I came to learn that the Union colonel whose coming frightened me out of the war and crippled the Southern cause to that extent; General Grant. I came within a few hours of seeing him when he was as unknown as I was myself; at a time when anybody could have said, 'Grant—Ulysses S. Grant? I do not remember hearing the name before.' It seems difficult to realize there was once a time when such a remark could be rationally made, but there was, I was within a few miles of the place and the occasion too, though proceeding in the other direction.

The thoughtful will not throw this war paper of mine lightly aside as being valueless. It has this value; it is not an unfair picture of what went on in may a militia camp in the first months of the rebellion, when the green recruits were without discipline, without the steadying and heartening influence of trained leaders, when all their circumstances were new and strange and charged with exaggerated terrors, and before the invaluable experience of actual collision in the field had turned them from rabbits into soldiers. If this side of the picture of that early day has not before been put into history, then history has been, to that degree incomplete, for it had and has its rightful place there. There was more Bull Run material scattered through the early camps of this country than exhibited itself at Bull Run. And yet, it learned it's trade presently and helped to fight the great battles later. I could have become a soldier myself if I had waited. I had got part of it learned, I knew more about retreating than the man that invented retreating.

11

LUCK

[Note—This is not a fancy sketch. I got it from a clergyman who was an instructor at Woolwich forty years ago, and who vouched for its truth.—M.T.]

It was at a banquet in London in honor of one of the two or three conspicuously illustrious English military names of this generation. For reasons which will presently appear, I will withhold his real name and titles, and call him Lieutenant General Lord Arthur Scoresby, V.C., K.C.B., etc., etc., etc. What a fascination there is in a renowned name! There sat the man, in actual flesh, whom I had heard of so many thousands of times since that day, thirty years before, when his name shot suddenly to the zenith from a Crimean battlefield, to remain forever celebrated. It was food and drink to me to look, and look, and look at that demigod; scanning, searching, noting: the quietness, the reserve, the noble gravity of his countenance; the simple honesty that expressed itself all over him; the sweet unconsciousness of his greatness—unconsciousness of the hundreds of admiring eyes fastened upon him, unconsciousness of the deep, loving, sincere worship welling out of the breasts of those people and flowing toward him.

The clergyman at my left was an old acquaintance of mine—clergyman now, but had spent the first half of his life in the camp and field, and as an instructor in the military school at Woolwich. Just at the moment I have been talking about, a veiled and singular light glimmered in his eyes, and he leaned down and muttered confidentially to me—indicating the hero of the banquet with a gesture:

'Privately—he's an absolute fool.'

This verdict was a great surprise to me. If its subject had been Napoleon, or Socrates, or Solomon, my astonishment could not have been greater. Two things I was well aware of: that the Reverend was a man of strict veracity, and that his judgement of men was good. Therefore I knew, beyond doubt or question, that the world was mistaken about this hero: he was a fool. So I meant to find out, at a convenient moment, how the Reverend, all solitary and alone, had discovered the secret.

Some days later the opportunity came, and this is what the Reverend told me.

About forty years ago I was an instructor in the military academy at Woolwich. I was present in one of the sections when young Scoresby underwent his preliminary examination. I was touched to the quick with pity; for the rest of the class answered up brightly and handsomely, while he—why, dear me, he didn't know anything, so to speak. He was evidently good, and sweet, and lovable, and guileless; and so it was exceedingly painful to see him stand there, as serene as a graven image, and deliver himself of answers which were veritably miraculous for stupidity and ignorance. All the compassion in me was aroused in his behalf. I said to myself, when he comes to be examined again, he will be flung over, of course; so it will be simply a harmless act of charity to ease his fall as much as I can. I took him aside, and found that he knew a little of Caesar's history; and as he didn't know anything else, I went to work and drilled him like a galley slave on a certain line of stock questions concerning Caesar which I knew would be used. If you'll believe me, he went through with flying colors on examination day! He went through on that purely superficial 'cram,' and got compliments too, while others, who knew a thousand times more than he, got plucked. By some strangely lucky accident—an accident not likely to happen twice in a century—he was asked no question outside of the narrow limits of his drill.

It was stupefying. Well, all through his course I stood by him, with something of the sentiment which a mother feels for a crippled child; and he always saved himself—just by miracle, apparently.

Now of course the thing that would expose him and kill him at last was mathematics. I resolved to make his death as easy as I could; so I drilled him and crammed him, and crammed him and drilled him, just on the line of questions which the examiners would be most likely to use, and then launching him on his fate. Well, sir, try to conceive of the result: to my consternation, he took the first prize! And with it he got a perfect ovation in the way of compliments.

Sleep? There was no more sleep for me for a week. My conscience tortured me day and night. What I had done I had done purely through charity, and only to ease the poor youth's fall—I never had dreamed of any such preposterous result as the thing that had happened. I felt as guilty and miserable as the creator of Frankenstein. Here was a woodenhead whom I had put in the way of glittering promotions and prodigious responsibilities, and but one thing could happen: he and his responsibilities would all go to ruin together at the first opportunity.

The Crimean war had just broken out. Of course there had to be a war, I said to myself: we couldn't have peace and give this donkey a chance to die before he is found out. I waited for the earthquake. It came. And it made me reel when it did come. He was actually gazetted to a captaincy in a marching regiment! Better men grow old and gray in the service before they climb to a sublimity like that. And who could ever have foreseen that they would go and put such a load of responsibility on such green and inadequate shoulders? I could just barely have stood it if they had made him a cornet; but a captain—think of it! I thought my hair would turn white.

Consider what I did—I who so loved repose and inaction. I said to myself, I am responsible to the country for this, and I must go along with him and protect the country against him as far as I can. So I took my poor little capital that I had saved up through years of work and grinding economy, and went with a sigh and bought a cornetcy in his regiment, and away we went to the field.

And there—oh dear, it was awful. Blunders? Why, he never did anything *but* blunder. But, you see, nobody was in the fellow's secret—everybody had him focused wrong, and necessarily misinterpreted his performance every time—consequently they took his idiotic blunders for inspirations of genius; they did, honestly! His mildest blunders were enough to make a man in his right mind cry; and they did make me cry—and rage and rave too, privately. And the thing that kept me always in a sweat of apprehension was the fact that every fresh blunder he made increased the luster of his reputation! I kept saying to myself, he'll get so high, that when discovery does finally come, it will be like the sun falling out of the sky.

He went right along up, from grade to grade, over the dead bodies of his superiors, until at last, in the hottest moment of the battle of—down went our colonel, and my heart jumped into my mouth, for Scoresby was next in rank! Now for it, said I; we'll all land in Sheol in ten minutes, sure.

The battle was awfully hot; the allies were steadily giving way all over the field. Our regiment occupied a position that was vital; a blunder now must be destruction. At this crucial moment, what does this immortal fool do but detach the regiment from its place and order a charge over a neighboring hill where there wasn't a suggestion of an enemy! 'There you go!' I said to myself; 'this is the end at last.'

And away we did go, and were over the shoulder of the hill before the insane movement could be discovered and stopped. And what did we find? An entire and unsuspected Russian army in reserve! And what happened? We were eaten up? That is necessarily what would have happened in ninety-nine cases out of a hundred. But no, those Russians argued that no single regiment would come browsing around there at such a time. It must be the entire English army, and that the sly Russian game was detected and blocked; so they turned tail, and away they went, pell-mell, over the hill and down into the field, in wild confusion, and we after them; they themselves broke the solid Russian center in the field, and tore through, and in no time there was the most tremendous rout you ever saw, and the defeat of the allies was turned into a sweeping and splendid victory! Marshal Canrobert looked on, dizzy with astonishment, admiration, and delight; and sent right off for Scoresby, and hugged him, and decorated him on the field, in presence of all the armies!

And what was Scoresby's blunder that time? Merely the mistaking his right hand for his left—that was all. An order had come to him to fall back and support our right; and instead, he fell forward and went over the hill to the left. But the name he won that day as a marvelous military genius filled the world with his glory, and that glory will never fade while history books last.

He is just as good and sweet and lovable and unpretending as a man can be, but he doesn't know enough to come in when it rains. Now that is absolutely true. He is the supremest ass in the universe; and until half an hour ago nobody knew it but himself and me. He has been pursued, day by day and year by year, by a most phenomenal and astonishing luckiness. He has been a shining soldier in all our wars for a generation; he has littered his whole military life with blunders, and yet has never committed one that didn't make him a knight or a baronet or a lord or something. Look at his breast; why, he is just clothed in domestic and foreign decorations. Well, sir, every one of them is the record of some shouting stupidity or other; and taken together, they are proof that the very best thing in all this world that can befall a man is to be born lucky. I say again, as I said at the banquet, Scoresby's an absolute fool.

12

ITALIAN WITHOUT A MASTER

It is almost a fortnight now that I am domiciled in a medieval villa in the country, a mile or two from Florence. I cannot speak the language; I am too old not to learn how, also too busy when I am busy, and too indolent when I am not; wherefore some will imagine that I am having a dull time of it. But it is not so. The 'help' are all natives; they talk Italian to me, I answer in English; I do not understand them, they do not understand me, consequently no harm is done, and everybody is satisfied. In order to be just and fair, I throw in an Italian word when I have one, and this has a good influence. I get the word out of the morning paper. I have to use it while it is fresh, for I find that Italian words do not keep in this climate. They fade toward night, and next morning they are gone. But it is no matter; I get a new one out of the paper before breakfast, and thrill the domestics with it while it lasts. I have no dictionary, and I do not want one; I can select words by the sound, or by orthographic aspect. Many of them have French or German or English look, and these are the ones I enslave for the day's service. That is, as a rule. Not always. If I find a learnable phrase that has an imposing look and warbles musically along I do not care to know the meaning of it; I pay it out to the first applicant, knowing that if I pronounce it carefully he will understand it, and that's enough.

Yesterday's word was avanti. It sounds Shakespearian, and

probably means Avaunt and quite my sight. Today I have a whole phrase: Sono dispiacentissimo. I do not know what it means, but it seems to fit in everywhere and give satisfaction. Although as a rule my words and phrases are good for one day and train only, I have several that stay by me all the time, for some unknown reason, and these come very handy when I get into a long conversation and need things to fire up with in monotonous stretches. One of the best ones is dov' `e il gatto. It nearly always produces a pleasant surprise, therefore I save it up for places where I want to express applause or admiration. The fourth word has a French sound, and I think the phrase means 'that takes the cake.'

During my first week in the deep and dreamy stillness of this woodsy and flowery place I was without news of the outside world, and was well content without it. It has been four weeks since I had seen a newspaper, and this lack seemed to give life a new charm and grace, and to saturate it with a feeling verging upon actual delight. Then came a change that was to be expected: the appetite for news began to rise again, after this invigorating rest. I had to feed it, but I was not willing to let it make me its helpless slave again; I determined to put it on a diet, and a strict and limited one. So I examined an Italian paper, with the idea of feeding it on that, and on that exclusively. On that exclusively, and without help of a dictionary. In this way I should surely be well protected against overloading and indigestion.

A glance at the telegraphic page filled me with encouragement. There were no scare-heads. That was good—supremely good. But there were headings—one-liners and two-liners—and that was good too; for without these, one must do as one does with a German paper—pay our precious time in finding out what an article is about, only to discover, in many cases, that there is nothing in it of interest to you. The headline is a valuable thing.

Necessarily we are all fond of murders, scandals, swindles, robberies, explosions, collisions, and all such things, when we knew the people, and when they are neighbors and friends, but when they are strangers we do not get any great pleasure out of them, as a rule. Now the trouble with an American paper is that it has no discrimination; it rakes the whole earth for blood and garbage, and the result is that you are daily overfed and suffer a surfeit. By habit you stow this muck every day, but you come by and by to take no vital interest in it—indeed, you almost get tired of it. As a rule, forty-nine-fiftieths of it concerns strangers only— people away off yonder, a thousand miles, two thousand miles, ten thousand miles from where you are. Why, when you come to think of it, who cares what becomes of those people? I would not give the assassination of one personal friend for a whole massacre of those others. And, to my mind, one relative or neighbor mixed up in a scandal is more interesting than a whole Sodom and Gomorrah of outlanders gone rotten. Give me the home product every time.

Very well. I saw at a glance that the Florentine paper would suit me: five out of six of its scandals and tragedies were local; they were adventures of one's very neighbors, one might almost say one's friends. In the matter of world news there was not too much, but just about enough. I subscribed. I have had no occasion to regret it. Every morning I get all the news I need for the day; sometimes from the headlines, sometimes from the text. I have never had to call for a dictionary yet. I read the paper with ease. Often I do not quite understand, often some of the details escape me, but no matter, I get the idea. I will cut out a passage or two, then you see how limpid the language is:

Il ritorno dei Beati d'Italia

Elargizione del Re all' Ospedale italiano

The first line means that the Italian sovereigns are coming back— they have been to England. The second line seems to mean that they enlarged the King at the Italian hospital. With a banquet, I suppose. An English banquet has that effect. Further:

Il ritorno dei Sovrani

a Roma

Roma, 24, ore 22,50.—I Sovrani e le Principessine Reali si attendono a Roma domani alle ore 15,51.

Return of the sovereigns to Rome, you see. Date of the telegram, Rome, November 24, ten minutes before twenty-three o'clock. The telegram seems to say, 'The Sovereigns and the Royal Children expect themselves at Rome tomorrow at fifty-one minutes after fifteen o'clock.'

I do not know about Italian time, but I judge it begins at midnight and runs through the twenty-four hours without breaking bulk. In the following ad, the theaters open at half-past twenty. If these are not matinees, 20.30 must mean 8.30 P.M., by my reckoning.

Spettacolli del di 25

Teatro della Pergola—(Ore 20,30)—Opera. Boh`eme. Teatro Alfieri.—Compagnia drammatica Drago—(Ore 20,30)— La Legge. Alhambra—(Ore 20,30)—Spettacolo variato. Sala Edison— Grandiosoo spettacolo Cinematografico: Quo Vadis?— Inaugurazione della Chiesa Russa—In coda al Direttissimo— Vedute di Firenze con gran movimeno—America: Transporto tronchi giganteschi—I ladri in casa del Diavolo—Scene comiche. Cinematografo—Via Brunelleschi n. 4.—Programma straordinario, Don Chisciotte—Prezzi populari.

The whole of that is intelligible to me—and sane and rational, too— except the remark about the Inauguration of a Russian Chinese. That one oversizes my hand. Give me five cards.

This is a four-page paper; and as it is set in long primer leaded and has a page of advertisements, there is no room for the crimes, disasters, and general sweepings of the outside world—thanks be! Today I find only a single importation of the off-color sort:

Una Principessa

che fugge con un cocchiere

Parigi, 24.—Il Matin ha da Berlino che la principessa Schovenbare-Waldenbure scomparve il 9 novembre. Sarebbe partita col suo cocchiere.

La Principassa ha 27 anni.

Twenty-seven years old, and scomparve—scampered—on the 9th November. You see by the added detail that she departed with her coachman. I hope Sarebbe has not made a mistake, but I am afraid the chances are that she has. Sono Dispiacentissimo.

There are several fires: also a couple of accidents. This is one of them:

Grave disgrazia sul Ponte Vecchio

Stammattina, circe le 7,30, mentre Giuseppe Sciatti, di anni 55, di Casellina e Torri, passava dal Ponte Vecchio, stando seduto sopra un barroccio carico di verdura, perse l' equilibrio e cadde al suolo, rimanendo con la gamba destra sotto una ruota del veicolo.

Lo Sciatti fu subito raccolto da alcuni cittadini, che, per mezzo della pubblica vettura n. 365, lo transportò a San Giovanni di Dio.

Ivi il medico di guardia gli riscontrò la frattura della gamba destra e alcune lievi escoriazioni giudicandolo guaribile in 50 giorni salvo complicazioni.

That it seems to say is this: 'Serious Disgrace on the Old Old Bridge. This morning about 7.30, Mr. Joseph Sciatti, aged 55, of Casellina and Torri, while standing up in a sitting posture on top of a carico barrow of vedure (foliage? hay? vegetables?), lost his equilibrium and fell on himself, arriving with his left leg under one of the wheels of the vehicle.

'Said Sciatti was suddenly harvested (gathered in?) by several citizens, who by means of public cab No. 365 transported to St. John of God.'

Paragraph No. 3 is a little obscure, but I think it says that the medico set the broken left leg—right enough, since there was nothing the matter with the other one—and that several are encouraged to hope that fifty days well fetch him around in quite giudicandolo-guaribile way, if no complications intervene.

I am sure I hope so myself.

There is a great and peculiar charm about reading news-scraps in a language which you are not acquainted with—the charm that always goes with the mysterious and the uncertain. You can never be absolutely sure of the meaning of anything you read in such circumstances; you are chasing an alert and gamy riddle all the time, and the baffling turns and dodges of the prey make the life of the hunt. A dictionary would spoil it. Sometimes a single word of doubtful purport will cast a veil of dreamy and golden uncertainty over a whole paragraph of cold and practical certainties, and leave steeped in a haunting and adorable mystery an incident which had been vulgar and commonplace but for that benefaction. Would you be wise to draw a dictionary on that gracious word? would you be properly grateful?

After a couple of days' rest I now come back to my subject and seek a case in point. I find it without trouble, in the morning paper; a cablegram from Chicago and Indiana by way of Paris. All the words save one are guessable by a person ignorant of Italian:

Revolverate in teatro

Parigi, 27.—La Patrie ha da Chicago:

Il guardiano del teatro dell'opera di Walace (Indiana), avendo voluto espellare uno spettatore che continuava a fumare malgrado il diviety, questo spalleggiato dai suoi amici tir'o diversi colpi di rivoltella. Il guardiano ripose. Nacque una scarica generale. Grande panico tra gli spettatori. Nessun ferito.

Translation.—'Revolveration in Theater. Paris, 27th. La Patrie has from Chicago: The cop of the theater of the opera of Wallace, Indiana, had willed to expel a spectator which continued to smoke in spite of the prohibition, who, spalleggiato by his friends, tir'o (Fr. tir'e, Anglice pulled) manifold revolver-shots; great panic among the spectators. Nobody hurt.'

It is bettable that that harmless cataclysm in the theater of the opera of Wallace, Indiana, excited not a person in Europe but me, and so came near to not being worth cabling to Florence by way of France. But it does excite me. It excites me because I cannot make out, for sure, what it was that moved the spectator to resist the officer. I was gliding along smoothly and without obstruction or accident, until I came to that word 'spalleggiato,' then the bottom fell out. You notice what a rich gloom, what a somber and pervading mystery, that word sheds all over the whole Wallachian tragedy. That is the charm of the thing, that is the delight of it. This is where you begin, this is where you revel. You can guess and guess, and have all the fun you like; you need not be afraid there will be an end to it; none is possible, for no amount of guessing will ever furnish you a meaning for that word that you can be sure is the right one. All the other words give you hints, by their form, their sound, or their spelling—this one doesn't, this one throws out no hints, this one keeps its secret. If there is even the slightest slight shadow of a hint anywhere, it lies in the very meagerly suggestive fact that 'spalleggiato' carries our word 'egg' in its stomach. Well, make the most out of it, and then where are you at? You conjecture that the spectator which was smoking in spite of the prohibition and become reprohibited by the guardians, was 'egged on' by his friends, and that was owing to that evil influence that he initiated the revolveration in theater that has galloped under the sea and come crashing through the European press without exciting anybody but me. But are you sure, are you dead sure, that that was the way of it? No. Then the uncertainty remains, the mystery abides, and with it the charm. Guess again.

If I had a phrase-book of a really satisfactory sort I would study it, and not give all my free time to undictionarial readings, but there is no such work on the market. The existing phrase-books are inadequate. They are well enough as far as they go, but when you fall down and skin your leg they don't tell you what to say.

13

A BURLESQUE BIOGRAPHY

Two or three persons having at different times intimated that if I would write an autobiography they would read it when they got leisure, I yield at last to this frenzied public demand and herewith tender my history.

Ours is a noble house, and stretches a long way back into antiquity. The earliest ancestor the Twains have any record of was a friend of the family by the name of Higgins. This was in the eleventh century, when our people were living in Aberdeen, county of Cork, England. Why it is that our long line has ever since borne the maternal name except when one of them now and then took a playful refuge in an alias to avert foolishness, instead of Higgins, is a mystery which none of us has ever felt much desire to stir. It is a kind of vague, pretty romance, and we leave it alone. All the old families do that way.

Arthur Twain was a man of considerable note—a solicitor on the highway in William Rufus's time. At about the age of thirty he went to one of those fine old English places of resort called Newgate, to see about something, and never returned again. While there he died suddenly.

Augustus Twain seems to have made something of a stir about the year 1160. He was as full of fun as he could be, and used to take his old saber and sharpen it up, and get in a convenient place on a dark night, and stick it through people as they went by, to see them jump. He was a born humorist. But he got to going too far with it; and the first time he was found stripping one of these parties, the authorities removed one end of him, and put it up on a nice high place on Temple Bar, where it could contemplate the people and have a good time. He never liked any situation so much or stuck to it so long.

Then for the next two hundred years the family tree shows a succession of soldiers—noble, high-spirited fellows, who always went into battle singing, right behind the army, and always went out whooping, right ahead of it.

This is a scathing rebuke to old dead Froissart's poor witticism that our family tree never had but one limb to it, and that that one stuck out at right angles, and bore fruit winter and summer.

Early in the fifteenth century we have Beau Twain, called 'the Scholar.' He wrote a beautiful, beautiful hand. And he could imitate anybody's hand so closely that it was enough to make a person laugh his head off to see it. He had infinite sport with his talent. But by and by he took a contract to break stone for a road, and the roughness of the work spoiled his hand. Still, he enjoyed life all the time he was in the stone business, which, with inconsiderable intervals, was some forty-two years. In fact, he died in harness. During all those long years he gave such satisfaction that he never was through with one contract a week till the government gave him another. He was a perfect pet. And he was always a favorite with his fellow-artists, and was a conspicuous member of their benevolent secret society, called the Chain Gang. He always wore his hair short, had a preference for striped clothes, and died lamented by the government. He was a sore loss to his country. For he was so regular.

Some years later we have the illustrious John Morgan Twain. He came over to this country with Columbus in 1492 as a passenger. He appears to have been of a crusty, uncomfortable disposition.

He complained of the food all the way over, and was always threatening to go ashore unless there was a change. He wanted fresh shad. Hardly a day passed over his head that he did not go idling about the ship with his nose in the air, sneering about the commander, and saying he did not believe Columbus knew where he was going to or had ever been there before. The memorable cry of 'Land ho!' thrilled every heart in the ship but his. He gazed awhile through a piece of smoked glass at the penciled line lying on the distant water, and then said: 'Land be hanged—it's a raft!'

When this questionable passenger came on board the ship, be brought nothing with him but an old newspaper containing a handkerchief marked 'B. G.,' one cotton sock marked 'L. W. C.,' one woolen one marked 'D. F.,' and a night-shirt marked 'O. M. R.' And yet during the voyage he worried more about his 'trunk,' and gave himself more airs about it, than all the rest of the passengers put together. If the ship was 'down by the head,' and would not steer, he would go and move his 'trunk' further aft, and then watch the effect. If the ship was 'by the stern,' he would suggest to Columbus to detail some men to 'shift that baggage.' In storms he had to be gagged, because his wailings about his 'trunk' made it impossible for the men to hear the orders. The man does not appear to have been openly charged with any gravely unbecoming thing, but it is noted in the ship's log as a 'curious circumstance' that albeit he brought his baggage on board the ship in a newspaper, he took it ashore in four trunks, a queensware crate, and a couple of champagne baskets. But when he came back insinuating, in an insolent, swaggering way, that some of this things were missing, and was going to search the other passengers' baggage, it was too much, and they threw him overboard. They watched long and wonderingly for him to come up, but not even a bubble rose on the quietly ebbing tide. But while every one was most absorbed in gazing over the side, and the interest was momentarily increasing, it was observed with consternation that the vessel was adrift and the anchor-cable hanging limp from the bow. Then in the ship's dimmed and ancient log we find this quaint note:

'In time it was discovered that the troblesome passenger hadde gone down and got the anchor, and took the same and sold it to the dam savages from the interior, saying the he had found it, the son of a gun!'

Yet this ancestor had good and noble instincts, and it is with pride that we call to mind the fact that he was the first white person who ever interested himself in the work of elevating and civilizing our Indians. He built a commodious jail and put up a gallows, and to his dying day he claimed with satisfaction that he had a more restraining and elevating influence on the Indians than any other reformer that ever labored among them. At this point the chronicle becomes less frank and chatty, and closes abruptly by saying that the old voyager went to see his gallows perform on the first white man ever hanged in America, and while there received injuries which terminated in his death.

The great-grandson of the 'Reformer' flourished in sixteen hundred and something, and was known in our annals as 'the old Admiral,' though in history he had other titles. He was long in command of fleets of swift vessels, well armed and manned, and did great service in hurrying up merchantmen. Vessels which he followed and kept his eagle eye on, always made good fair time across the ocean. But if a ship still loitered in spite of all he could do, his indignation would grow till he could contain himself no longer— and then he would take that ship home where he lived and keep it there carefully, expecting the owners to come for it, but they never did. And he would try to get the idleness and sloth out of the sailors of that ship by compelling them to take invigorating exercise and a bath. He called it 'walking a plank.' All the pupils liked it. At any rate, they never found any fault with it after trying it. When the owners were late coming for their ships, the Admiral always burned them, so that the insurance money should not be lost. At last this fine old tar was cut down in the fullness of his years and honors. And to her dying day, his poor heart-broken widow believed that if he had been cut down fifteen minutes sooner he might have been resuscitated.

Charles Henry Twain lived during the latter part of the seventeenth century, and was a zealous and distinguished missionary. He converted sixteen thousand South Sea islanders, and taught them that a dog-tooth necklace and a pair of spectacles was not enough clothing to come to divine service in. His poor flock loved him very, very dearly; and when his funeral was over, they got up in a body and came out of the restaurant with tears in their eyes, and saying, one to another, that he was a good tender missionary, and they wished they had some more of him.

Pah-go-to-wah-wah-pukketekeewis Mighty-Hunter-with-a-Hog-Eye-Twain adorned the middle of the eighteenth century, and aided General Braddock with all his heart to resist the oppressor Washington. It was this ancestor who fired seventeen times at our Washington from behind a tree. So far the beautiful romantic narrative in the moral story-books is correct; but when that narrative goes on to say that at the seventeenth round the awe-stricken savage said solemnly that that man was being reserved by the Great Spirit for some mighty mission, and he dared not lift his sacrilegious rifle against him again, the narrative seriously impairs the integrity of history. What he did say was:

'It ain't no hic no use. 'At man's so drunk he can't stan' still long enough for a man to hit him. I hic I can't 'ford to fool away any more am'nition on him.'

That was why he stopped at the seventeenth round, and it was a good, plain, matter-of-fact reason, too, and one that easily commends itself to us by the eloquent, persuasive flavor of probability there is about it.

I also enjoyed the story-book narrative, but I felt a marring misgiving that every Indian at Braddock's Defeat who fired at a soldier a couple of times two easily grows to seventeen in a century, and missed him, jumped to the conclusion that the Great Spirit was reserving that soldier for some grand mission; and so I somehow feared that the only reason why Washington's case is remembered and the others forgotten is, that in his the prophecy came true, and in that of the others it didn't. There are not books enough on earth to contain the record of the prophecies Indians and other unauthorized parties have made; but one may carry in his overcoat pockets the record of all the prophecies that have been fulfilled.

I will remark here, in passing, that certain ancestors of mine are so thoroughly well-known in history by their aliases, that I have not felt it to be worth while to dwell upon them, or even mention them in the order of their birth. Among these may be mentioned Richard Brinsley Twain, alias Guy Fawkes; John Wentworth Twain, alias Sixteen-String Jack; William Hogarth Twain, alias Jack Sheppard; Ananias Twain, alias Baron Munchausen; John George Twain, alias Captain Kydd; and then there are George Francis Twain, Tom Pepper, Nebuchadnezzar, and Baalam's Ass—they all belong to our family, but to a branch of it somewhat distinctly removed from the honorable direct line—in fact, a collateral branch, whose members chiefly differ from the ancient stock in that, in order to acquire the notoriety we have always yearned and hungered for, they have got into a low way of going to jail instead of getting hanged.

It is not well, when writing an autobiography, to follow your ancestry down too close to your own time—it is safest to speak only vaguely of your great-grandfather, and then skip from there to yourself, which I now do.

I was born without teeth—and there Richard III. had the advantage of me; but I was born without a humpback, likewise, and there I had the advantage of him. My parents were neither very poor nor conspicuously honest.

But now a thought occurs to me. My own history would really seem so tame contrasted with that of my ancestors, that it is simply wisdom to leave it unwritten until I am hanged. If some other biographies I have read had stopped with the ancestry until a like event occurred, it would have been a felicitous thing for the reading public. How does it strike you?

14

THE CELEBRATED JUMPING FROG
OF CALAVERAS COUNTY

In compliance with the request of a friend of mine, who wrote me from the East, I called on good-natured, garrulous old Simon Wheeler, and inquired after my friend's friend, Leonidas W. Smiley, as requested to do, and I hereunto append the result. I have a lurking suspicion that Leonidas W. Smiley is a myth; that my friend never knew such a personage; and that he only conjectured that, if I asked old Wheeler about him, it would remind him of his infamous Jim Smiley, and he would go to work and bore me nearly to death with some infernal reminiscence of him as long and tedious as it should be useless to me. If that was the design, it certainly suceeded.

I found Simon Wheeler dozing comfortably by the barroom stove of the old, dilapidated tavern in the ancient mining camp of Angel's, and I noticed that he was fat and bald-headed, and had an expression of winning gentleness and simplicity upon his tranquil countenance. He roused up and gave me good-day. I told him a friend of mine had commissioned me to make some inquiries about a cherished companion of his boyhood named Leonidas W. Smiley—Rev. Leonidas W. Smiley—a young minister of the Gospel, who he had heard was at one time a resident of Angel's

Camp. I added that, if Mr. Wheeler could tell me anything about this Rev. Leonidas W. Smiley, I would feel under many obligations to him.

Simon Wheeler backed me into a corner and blockaded me there with his chair, and then sat me down and reeled off the monotonous narrative which follows this paragraph. He never smiled, he never frowned, he never changed his voice from the gentle-flowing key to which he tuned the initial sentence, he never betrayed the slightest suspicion of enthusiasm; but all through the interminable narrative there ran a vein of impressive earnestness and sincerity, which showed me plainly that, so far from his imagining that there was anything ridiculous or funny about his story, he regarded it as a really important matter, and admired its two heroes as men of transcendent genius in finesse. To me, the spectacle of a man drifting serenely along through such a queer yarn without ever smiling, was exquisitely absurd. As I said before, I asked him to tell me what he knew of Rev. Leonidas W. Smiley, and he replied as follows. I let him go on in his own way, and never interrupted him once:

There was a feller here once by the name of Jim Smiley, in the winter of '49—or maybe it was the spring of '50—I don't recollect exactly, somehow, though what makes me think it was one or the other is because I remember the big flume wasn't finished when he first came to the camp; but anyway, he was the curiousest man about always betting on anything that turned up you ever see, if he could get anybody to bet on the other side; and if he couldn't, he'd change sides. Any way that suited the other man would suit him—any way just so's he got a bet, he was satisfied. But still he was lucky, uncommon lucky; he most always come out winner. He was always ready and laying for a chance; there couldn't be no solit'ry thing mentioned but that feller'd offer to bet on it, and take any side you please, as I was just telling you. If there was a horse race, you'd find him flush, or you'd find him busted at the end of it; if there was a dogfight, he'd bet on it; if there was a cat-fight, he'd bet on it; if there was a chicken-fight, he'd bet on it; why, if there was two birds setting on a fence, he would bet you which one would fly first; or if there was a camp meeting, he would be there reg'lar, to bet on Parson Walker, which he judged to be the best exhorter about here, and so he was, too, and a good man. If he even seen a straddlebug start to go anywheres, he would bet you how long it would take him to get wherever he was going to, and if you took him up, he would foller that straddlebug to Mexico but what he would find out where he was bound for and how long he was on the road. Lots of the boys here has seen that Smiley, and can tell you about him. Why, it never made no difference to him— he would bet on anything—the dangdest feller. Parson Walker's wife laid very sick once, for a good while, and it seemed as if they warn't going to save her; but one morning he come in, and Smiley asked ho! ! who she was, and he said she was considerable better—thank the Lord for his inf'nit mercy—and coming on so smart that, with the blessing of Prov'dence, she'd get well yet; and Smiley, before he thought, says, 'Well, I'll risk two-and-a-half that she don't, anyway.'

Thish-yer Smiley had a mare—the boys called her the fifteen-minute nag, but that was only in fun, you know, because, of course, she was faster than that—and he used to win money on that horse, for all she was so slow and always had the asthma, or the distemper, or the consumption, or something of that kind. They used to give her two or three hundred yards start, and then pass her under way; but always at the fag end of the race she'd get excited and desperate-like, and come cavorting and straddling up, and scattering her legs around limber, sometimes in the air, and sometimes out to one side amongst the fences, and kicking up more dust, and raising more racket with her coughing and sneezing and blowing her nose—and always fetch up at the stand just about a neck ahead, as near as you could cipher it down.

And he had a little small bull pup, that to look at him you'd think he wan't worth a cent, but to set around and look ornery, and lay for a chance to steal something. But as soon as money was up on him, he was a different dog; his underjaw'd begin to stick out like the fo-castle of a steamboat, and his teeth would uncover, and shine savage like the furnaces. And a dog might tackle him, and bully-rag him, and bite him, and throw him over his shoulder two or three times, and Andrew Jackson—which was the name of the pup—Andrew Jackson would never let on but what he was satisfied, and hadn't expected nothing else—and the bets being doubled and doubled on the other side all the time, till the money was all up; and then all of a sudden he would grab that other dog jest by the j'int of his hind leg and freeze to it—not chaw, you understand, but only jest grip and hang on till they throwed up the sponge, if it was a year. Smiley always come out winner on that pup, till he harnessed a dog once that didn't have no hind legs, because they'd been sawed off by a circular saw, and when the thing had gone along far enough, and the money was all up, and he come to make a snatch for his pet holt, he saw in a minute how he'd been imposed on, and how the other dog had him in the door, so to speak, and he 'peared surprised, and then he looked sorter discouraged-like, and didn't try no more to win the fight, and so he got shucked out bad. He give Smiley a look, as much as to say his heart was broke, and it was his fault for putting up a dog that hadn't no hind legs for him to take holt of, which was his main dependence in a fight, and then he limped off a piece and laid down and died. It was a good pup, was that Andrew Jackson, and would have made a name for hisself if he'd lived, for the stuff was in him, and he had genius—I know it, because he hadn't had no opportunities to speak of, and it don't stand to reason that a dog could make such a fight as he could under them circumstances, if he hadn't no talent. It always makes me feel sorry when I think of that last fight of his', and the way it turned out.

Well, thish-yer Smiley had rat-tarriers, and chicken cocks, and tomcats, and all them kind of things, till you couldn't rest, and you couldn't fetch nothing for him to bet on but he'd match you. He ketched a frog one day, and took him home, and said he cal'klated to edercate him; and so he never done nothing for three months but set in his back yard and learn that frog to jump. And you bet you he did learn him too. He'd give him a little punch behind, and the next minute you'd see that frog whirling in the air like a doughnut—see him turn one summerset, or may be a couple, if he got a good start, and come down flatfooted and all right, like a cat. He got him up so in the matter of catching flies, and kept him in practice so constant, that he'd nail a fly every time as far as he could see him. Smiley said all a frog wanted was education, and he could do most anything—and I believe him. Why, I've seen him set Dan'l Webster down here on this floor—Dan'l Webster was the name of the frog—and sing out, 'Flies, Dan'l, flies!' and quicker'n you could wink, he'd spring straight up, and snake a fly off'n the counter there, and flop down on the floor again as solid as a gob of mud, and fall to scratching the side of his head with his hind foot as indifferent as if he hadn't no idea he'd been doin' any more' any frog might do. You never see a frog so modest and straightfor'ard as he was, for all he was so gifted. And when it came to fair and square jumping on a dead level, he could get over more ground at one straddle than any animal of his breed you ever see. Jumping on a dead level was his strong suit, you understand; and when it come to that, Smiley would ante up money on him as long as he had a red. Smiley was monstrous proud of his frog, and well he might be, for fellers that had traveled and been everywheres, all said he laid over any frog that ever they see.

Well, Smiley kept the beast in a little lattice box, and he used to fetch him downtown sometimes and lay for a bet. One day a feller—a stranger in the camp, he was—come across him with his box, and says:

'What might it be that you've got in the box?'

And Smiley says, sorter indifferent like, 'It might be a parrot, or it might be a canary, maybe, but it an't—it's only just a frog.'

And the feller took it, and looked at it careful, and turned it round this way and that, and says, 'H'm—so 'tis. Well, what's he good for?'

'Well,' Smiley says, easy and careless, 'he's good enough for one thing, I should judge—he can outjump any frog in Calaveras county.'

The feller took the box again, and took another long, particular look, and give it back to Smiley, and says, very deliberate, 'Well, I don't see no p'ints about that frog that's any better'n any other frog.'

'Maybe you don't,' Smiley says. 'Maybe you understand frogs, and maybe you don't understand 'em; maybe you've had experience, and maybe you an't only a amature, as it were. Anyways, I've got my opinion, and I'll risk forty dollars that he can outjump any frog in Calaveras county.'

And the feller studied a minute, and then says, kinder sad like, 'Well, I'm only a stranger here, and I an't got no frog; but if I had a frog, I'd bet you.'

And then Smiley says, 'That's all right—that's all right—if you'll hold my box a minute, I'll go and get you a frog.' And so the feller took the box, and put up his forty dollars along with Smiley's and set down to wait.

So he sat there a good while thinking and thinking to himself, and then he got the frog out and prized his mouth open and took a teaspoon and filled him full of quail shot—filled him pretty near up to his chin—and set him on the floor. Smiley he went to the swamp and slopped around in the mud for a long time, and finally he ketched a frog, and fetched him in, and give him to this feller, and says:

'Now, if you're ready, set him alongside of Dan'l, with his

fore-paws just even with Dan'l and I'll give the word.' Then he says, 'one—two—three—jump!' and him and the feller touched up the frogs from behind, and the new frog hopped off, but Dan'l gave a heave, and hysted up his shoulders—so—like a French-man, but it wan't no use—he couldn't budge; he was planted as solid as an anvil, and he couldn't no more stir than if he was anchored out. Smiley was a good deal surprised, and he was disgusted too, but he didn't have no idea what the matter was, of course.

The feller took the money and started away; and when he was going out at the door, he sort of jerked his thumb over his shoulders—this way—at Dan'l, and says again, very deliberate, 'Well, I don't see no p'ints about that frog that's any better'n any other frog.'

Smiley he stood scratching his head and looking down at Dan'l a long time, and at last he says, 'I do wonder what in the nation that frog throw'd off for—I wonder if there an't something the matter with him—he 'pears to look might baggy, somehow.' And he ketched Dan'l by the nap of the neck, and lifted him up and says, 'Why, blame my cats, if he don't weigh five pound!' and turned him upside down, and he belched out a double handful of shot. And then he see how it was, and he was the maddest man—he set the frog down and took out after that feller, but he never ketched him. And—

[Here Simon Wheeler heard his name called from the front yard, and got up to see what was wanted.] And turning to me as he moved away, he said: 'Just set where you are, stranger, and rest easy—I an't going to be gone a second.'

But, by your leave, I did not think that a continuation of the history of the enterprising vagabond Jim Smiley would be likely to afford me much information concerning the Rev. Leonidas W. Smiley, and so I started away.

At the door I met the sociable Wheeler returning, and he buttonholed me and recommenced:

Well, thish-yer Smiley had a yaller one-eyed cow that didn't have no tail, only jest a short stump like a bannanner, and—'

'Oh! hang Smiley and his afflicted cow!' I muttered, good-naturedly, and bidding the old gentleman good-day, I departed.

15

WAS IT HEAVEN? OR HELL?

CHAPTER I

'You told a LIE?'

'You confess it—you actually confess it—you told a lie!'

CHAPTER II

The family consisted of four persons: Margaret Lester, widow, aged thirty six; Helen Lester, her daughter, aged sixteen; Mrs. Lester's maiden aunts, Hannah and Hester Gray, twins, aged sixty-seven. Waking and sleeping, the three women spent their days and night in adoring the young girl; in watching the movements of her sweet spirit in the mirror of her face; in refreshing their souls with the vision of her bloom and beauty; in listening to the music of her voice; in gratefully recognizing how rich and fair for them was the world with this presence in it; in shuddering to think how desolate it would be with this light gone out of it.

By nature—and inside—the aged aunts were utterly dear and lovable and good, but in the matter of morals and conduct their training had been so uncompromisingly strict that it had made them exteriorly austere, not to say stern. Their influence was effective in the house; so effective that the mother and the daughter conformed to its moral and religious requirements cheerfully, contentedly, happily, unquestionably. To do this was become second nature to them. And so in this peaceful heaven there were no clashings, no irritations, no fault-finding, no heart-burnings. In it a lie had no place. In it a lie was unthinkable. In it speech was restricted to absolute truth, iron-bound truth, implacable and uncompromising truth, let the resulting consequences be what they might. At last, one day, under stress of circumstances, the darling of the house sullied her lips with a lie—and confessed it, with tears and self-upbraidings. There are not any words that can paint the consternation of the aunts. It was as if the sky had crumpled up and collapsed and the earth had tumbled to ruin with a crash. They sat side by side, white and stern, gazing speechless upon the culprit, who was on her knees before them with her face buried first in one lap and then the other, moaning and sobbing, and appealing for sympathy and forgiveness and getting no response, humbly kissing the hand of the one, then of the other, only to see it withdrawn as suffering defilement by those soiled lips.

Twice, at intervals, Aunt Hester said, in frozen amazement: 'You told a LIE?' Twice, at intervals, Aunt Hannah followed with the muttered and amazed ejaculation: 'You confess it—you actually confess it—you told a lie!'

It was all they could say. The situation was new, unheard of, incredible; they could not understand it, they did not know how to take hold of it, it approximately paralyzed speech.

At length it was decided that the erring child must be taken to her mother, who was ill, and who ought to know what had happened. Helen begged, besought, implored that she might be spared this further disgrace, and that her mother might be spared the grief and pain of it; but this could not be: duty required this sacrifice, duty takes precedence of all things, nothing can absolve one from a duty, with a duty no compromise is possible.

Helen still begged, and said the sin was her own, her mother had had no hand in it—why must she be made to suffer for it? But the aunts were obdurate in their righteousness, and said the law that visited the sins of the parent upon the child was by all right and reason reversible; and, therefore, it was but just that the innocent mother of a sinning child should suffer her rightful share of the grief and pain and shame which were the allotted wages of the sin.

The three moved toward the sick-room. At this time the doctor was approaching the house. He was still a good distance away, however. He was a good doctor and a good man, and he had a good heart, but one had to know him a year to get over hating him, two years to learn to endure him, three to learn to like him, and four and five to learn to love him. It was a slow and trying education, but it paid. He was of great stature; he had a leonine head, a leonine face, a rough voice, and an eye which was sometimes a pirate's and sometimes a woman's, according to the mood. He knew nothing about etiquette, and cared nothing about it; in speech, manner, carriage, and conduct he was the reverse of conventional. He was frank, to the limit; he had opinions on all subjects; they were always on tap and ready for delivery, and he cared not a farthing whether his listener liked them or didn't. Whom he loved he loved, and manifested it; whom he didn't love he hated, and published it from the housetops. In his young days he had been a sailor, and the salt-airs of all the seas blew from him yet. He was a sturdy and loyal Christian, and believed he was the best one in the land, and the only one whose Christianity was perfectly sound, healthy, full-charged with common sense, and had no decayed places in it. People who had an axe to grind, or people who for any reason wanted to get on the soft side of him, called him The Christian—a phrase whose delicate flattery was music to his ears, and whose capital T was such an enchanting and vivid object to him that he could SEE it when it fell out of a person's mouth even in the dark. Many who were fond of him stood on their consciences with both feet and brazenly called him by that large title habitually, because it was a pleasure to them to do anything that would please him; and with eager and cordial malice his extensive and diligently cultivated crop of enemies gilded it, beflowered it, expanded it to 'The ONLY Christian.' Of these two titles, the latter had the wider currency; the enemy, being greatly in the majority, attended to that. Whatever the doctor believed, he believed with all his heart, and would fight for it whenever he got the chance; and if the intervals between chances grew to be irksomely wide, he would invent ways of shortening them himself. He was severely conscientious, according to his rather independent lights, and whatever he took to be a duty he performed, no matter whether the judgment of the professional moralists agreed with his own or not. At sea, in his young days, he had used profanity freely, but as soon as he was converted he made a rule, which he rigidly stuck to ever afterward, never to use it except on the rarest occasions, and then only when duty commanded. He had been a hard drinker at sea, but after his conversion he became a firm and outspoken teetotaler, in order to be an example to the young, and from that time forth he seldom drank; never, indeed, except when it seemed to him to be a duty—a condition which sometimes occurred a couple of times a year, but never as many as five times.

Necessarily, such a man is impressionable, impulsive, emotional. This one was, and had no gift at hiding his feelings; or if he had it he took no trouble to exercise it. He carried his soul's prevailing weather in his face, and when he entered a room the parasols or the umbrellas went up—figuratively speaking—according to the indications. When the soft light was in his eye it meant approval, and delivered a benediction; when he came with a frown he lowered the temperature ten degrees. He was a well-beloved man in the house of his friends, but sometimes a dreaded one. He had a deep affection for the Lester household and its several members returned this feeling with interest. They mourned over his kind of Christianity, and he frankly scoffed at theirs; but both parties went on loving each other just the same.

He was approaching the house—out of the distance; the aunts and the culprit were moving toward the sick-chamber.

CHAPTER III

The three last named stood by the bed; the aunts austere, the transgressor softly sobbing. The mother turned her head on the pillow; her tired eyes flamed up instantly with sympathy and passionate mother-love when they fell upon her child, and she opened the refuge and shelter of her arms.

'Wait!' said Aunt Hannah, and put out her hand and stayed the girl from leaping into them.

'Helen,' said the other aunt, impressively, 'tell your mother all. Purge your soul; leave nothing unconfessed.'

Standing stricken and forlorn before her judges, the young girl mourned her sorrowful tale through the end, then in a passion of appeal cried out : 'Oh, mother, can't you forgive me? won't you forgive me?—I am so desolate!'

'Forgive you, my darling? Oh, come to my arms!—there, lay your head upon my breast, and be at peace. If you had told a thousand lies—'

There was a sound—a warning—the clearing of a throat. The aunts glanced up, and withered in their clothes—there stood the doctor, his face a thunder-cloud. Mother and child knew nothing of his presence; they lay locked together, heart to heart, steeped in immeasurable content, dead to all things else. The physician stood many moments glaring and glooming upon the scene before him; studying it, analyzing it, searching out its genesis; then he put up his hand and beckoned to the aunts. They came trembling to him, and stood humbly before him and waited. He bent down and whispered: 'Didn't I tell you this patient must be protected from all excitement? What the hell have you been doing? Clear out of the place!'

They obeyed. Half an hour later he appeared in the parlor,

serene, cheery, clothed in sunshine, conducting Helen, with his arm about her waist, petting her, and saying gentle and playful things to her; and she also was her sunny and happy self again.

'Now, then,' he said, 'good-bye, dear. Go to your room, and keep away from your mother, and behave yourself. But wait—put out your tongue. There, that will do—you're as sound as a nut!' He patted her cheek and added, 'Run along now; I want to talk to these aunts.'

She went from the presence. His face clouded over again at once; and as he sat down he said: 'You too have been doing a lot of damage—and maybe some good. Some good, yes—such as it is. That woman's disease is typhoid! You've brought it to a show-up, I think, with your insanities, and that's a service—such as it is. I hadn't been able to determine what it was before.'

With one impulse the old ladies sprang to their feet, quaking with terror. 'Sit down! What are you proposing to do?'

'Do? We must fly to her. We—'

'You'll do nothing of the kind; you've done enough harm for one day. Do you want to squander all your capital of crimes and follies on a single deal? Sit down, I tell you. I have arranged for her to sleep; she needs it; if you disturb her without my orders, I'll brain you—if you've got the materials for it.'

They sat down, distressed and indignant, but obedient, under compulsion. He proceeded: 'Now, then, I want this case explained. THEY wanted to explain it to me—as if there hadn't been emotion or excitement enough already. You knew my orders; how did you dare to go in there and get up that riot?'

Hester looked appealing at Hannah; Hannah returned a beseeching look at Hester—neither wanted to dance to this unsympathetic orchestra. The doctor came to their help. He said: 'Begin, Hester.' Fingering at the fringes of her shawl, and with lowered eyes, Hester said, timidly: 'We should not have disobeyed for any ordinary cause, but this was vital. This was a duty. With a duty one has no choice; one must put all lighter considerations aside and perform it. We were obliged to arraign her before her mother. She had told a lie.'

The doctor glowered upon the woman a moment, and seemed to be trying to work up in his mind an understand of a wholly incomprehensible proposition; then he stormed out: 'She told a lie! DID she? God bless my soul! I tell a million a day!

And so does every doctor. And so does everybody—including you—for that matter. And THAT was the important thing that authorized you to venture to disobey my orders and imperil that woman's life! Look here, Hester Gray, this is pure lunacy; that girl COULDN'T tell a lie that was intended to injure a person. The thing is impossible—absolutely impossible. You know it yourselves—both of you; you know it perfectly well.'

Hannah came to her sister's rescue: 'Hester didn't mean that it was that kind of a lie, and it wasn't. But it was a lie.'

'Well, upon my word, I never heard such nonsense! Haven't you got sense enough to discriminate between lies! Don't you know the difference between a lie that helps and a lie that hurts?'

'ALL lies are sinful,' said Hannah, setting her lips together like a vise; 'all lies are forbidden.'

The Only Christian fidgeted impatiently in his chair. He went to attack this proposition, but he did not quite know how or where to begin.Finally he made a venture: 'Hester, wouldn't you tell a lie to shield a person from an undeserved injury or shame?'

'No.'

'Not even a friend?'

'No.'

'Not even your dearest friend?'

'No. I would not.'

The doctor struggled in silence awhile with this situation; then he asked: 'Not even to save him from bitter pain and misery and grief?'

'No. Not even to save his life.'

Another pause. Then: 'Nor his soul?'

There was a hush—a silence which endured a measurable interval—then Hester answered, in a low voice, but with decision: 'Nor his soul?'

No one spoke for a while; then the doctor said: 'Is it with you the same, Hannah?'

'Yes,' she answered.

'I ask you both—why?'

'Because to tell such a lie, or any lie, is a sin, and could cost us the loss of our own souls—WOULD, indeed, if we died without time to repent.'

'Strange... strange... it is past belief.' Then he asked, roughly: 'Is such a soul as that WORTH saving?' He rose up, mumbling and grumbling, and started for the door, stumping vigorously along. At the threshold he turned and rasped out an admonition: 'Reform! Drop this mean and sordid and selfish devotion to the saving of your shabby little souls, and hunt up something to do that's got some dignity to it! RISK your souls! Risk them in good causes; then if you lose them, why should you care? Reform!'

The good old gentlewomen sat paralyzed, pulverized, outraged, insulted, and brooded in bitterness and indignation over these blasphemies. They were hurt to the heart, poor old ladies, and said they could never forgive these injuries.

'Reform!'

They kept repeating that word resentfully. 'Reform—and learn to tell lies!'

Time slipped along, and in due course a change came over their spirits. They had completed the human being's first duty—which is to think about himself until he has exhausted the subject, then he is in a condition to take up minor interests and think of other people. This changes the complexion of his spirits—generally wholesomely. The minds of the two old ladies reverted to their beloved niece and the fearful disease which had smitten her; instantly they forgot the hurts their self-love had received, and a passionate desire rose in their hearts to go to the help of the sufferer and comfort her with their love, and minister to her, and labor for her the best they could with their weak hands, and joyfully and affectionately wear out their poor old bodies in her dear service if only they might have the privilege.

'And we shall have it!' said Hester, with the tears running down her face. 'There are no nurses comparable to us, for there are no others that will stand their watch by that bed till they drop and die, and God knows we would do that.'

'Amen,' said Hannah, smiling approval and endorsement through the mist of moisture that blurred her glasses. 'The doctor knows us, and knows we will not disobey again; and he will call no others. He will not dare!'

'Dare?' said Hester, with temper, and dashing the water from her eyes; 'he will dare anything—that Christian devil! But it will do no good for him to try it this time—but, laws! Hannah! after all's said and done, he is gifted and wise and good, and he would not think of such a thing.... It is surely time for one of us to go to that room. What is keeping him? Why doesn't he come and say so?'

They caught the sound of his approaching step. He entered, sat down, and began to talk.

'Margaret is a sick woman,' he said. 'She is still sleeping, but she will wake presently; then one of you must go to her. She will be worse before she is better. Pretty soon a night-and-day watch must be set. How much of it can you two undertake?'

'All of it!' burst from both ladies at once.

The doctor's eyes flashed, and he said, with energy: 'You DO ring true, you brave old relics! And you SHALL do all of the nursing you can, for there's none to match you in that divine office in his town; but you can't do all of it, and it would be a crime to let you.' It was grand praise, golden praise, coming from such a source, and it took nearly all the resentment out of the aged twin's hearts. 'Your Tilly and my old Nancy shall do the rest—good nurses both, white souls with black skins, watchful, loving, tender—just perfect nurses!—and competent liars from the cradle.... Look you! keep a little watch on Helen; she is sick, and is going to be sicker.'

The ladies looked a little surprised, and not credulous; and Hester said: 'How is that? It isn't an hour since you said she was as sound as anut.'

The doctor answered, tranquilly: 'It was a lie.'

The ladies turned upon him indignantly, and Hannah said: 'How can you make an odious confession like that, in so indifferent a tone, when you know how we feel about all forms of—'

'Hush! You are as ignorant as cats, both of you, and you don't know what you are talking about. You are like all the rest of the moral moles; you lie from morning till night, but because you don't do it with your mouths, but only with your lying eyes, your lying inflections, your deceptively misplaced emphasis, and your misleading gestures, you turn up your complacent noses and parade before God and the world as saintly and unsmirched Truth-Speakers, in whose cold-storage souls a lie would freeze to death if it got there! Why will you humbug yourselves with that foolish notion that no lie is a lie except a spoken one? What is the difference between lying with your eyes and lying with your mouth? There is none; and if you would reflect a moment you would see that it is so. There isn't a human being that doesn't tell a gross of lies every day of his life; and you—why, between you, you tell thirty thousand; yet you flare up here in a lurid hypocritical horror because I tell that child a benevolent and sinless lie to protect her from her imagination, which would get to work and warm up her blood to a fever in an hour, if I were disloyal enough to my duty to let it. Which I should probably do if I were interested in saving my soul by such disreputable means.

'Come, let us reason together. Let us examine details. When you two were in the sick-room raising that riot, what would you have done if you had known I was coming?'

'Well, what?'

'You would have slipped out and carried Helen with you—wouldn't you?'

The ladies were silent.

'What would be your object and intention?'

'Well, what?'

'To keep me from finding out your guilt; to beguile me to infer that Margaret's excitement proceeded from some cause not known to you. In a word, to tell me a lie—a silent lie. Moreover, a possibly harmful one.'

The twins colored, but did not speak 'You not only tell myriads of silent lies, but you tell lies with your mouths—you two.'

'THAT is not so!'

'It is so. But only harmless ones. You never dream of uttering a harmful one. Do you know that that is a concession—and a confession?'

'How do you mean?'

'It is an unconscious concession that harmless lies are not criminal; it is a confession that you constantly MAKE that discrimination. For instance, you declined old Mrs. Foster's invitation last week to meet those odious Higbies at supper—in a polite note in which you expressed regret and said you were very sorry you could not go. It was a lie.

It was as unmitigated a lie as was ever uttered. Deny it, Hester—with another lie.'

Hester replied with a toss of her head.

'That will not do. Answer. Was it a lie, or wasn't it?'

The color stole into the cheeks of both women, and with a struggle and an effort they got out their confession: 'It was a lie.'

'Good—the reform is beginning; there is hope for you yet; you will not tell a lie to save your dearest friend's soul, but you will spew out one without a scruple to save yourself the discomfort of telling an unpleasant truth.'

He rose. Hester, speaking for both, said; coldly: 'We have lied; we perceive it; it will occur no more. To lie is a sin.

We shall never tell another one of any kind whatsoever, even lies of courtesy or benevolence, to save any one a pang or a sorrow decreed for him by God.'

'Ah, how soon you will fall! In fact, you have fallen already; for what you have just uttered is a lie. Good-bye. Reform! One of you go to the sick-room now.'

CHAPTER IV

Twelve days later. Mother and child were lingering in the grip of the hideous disease. Of hope for either there was little. The aged sisters looked white and worn, but they would not give up their posts. Their hearts were breaking, poor old things, but their grit was steadfast and indestructible. All the twelve days the mother had pined for the child, and the child for the mother, but both knew that the prayer of these longings could not be granted. When the mother was told—on the first day—that her disease was typhoid, she was frightened, and asked if there was danger that Helen could have contracted it the day before, when she was in the sick-chamber on that confession visit. Hester told her the doctor had poo-pooed the idea. It troubled Hester to say it, although it was true, for she had not believed the doctor; but when she saw the mother's joy in the news, the pain in her conscience lost something of its force—a result which made her ashamed of the constructive deception which she had practiced, though not ashamed enough to make her distinctly and definitely wish she had refrained from it. From that moment the sick woman understood that her daughter must remain away, and she said she would reconcile herself to the separation the best she could, for she would rather suffer death than have her child's health imperiled. That afternoon Helen had to take to her bed, ill. She grew worse during the night.

In the morning her mother asked after her: 'Is she well?' Hester turned cold; she opened her lips, but the words refused to come. The mother lay languidly looking, musing, waiting; suddenly she turned white and gasped out: 'Oh, my God! what is it? Is she sick?'

Then the poor aunt's tortured heart rose in rebellion, and words came: 'No—be comforted; she is well.'

The sick woman put all her happy heart in her gratitude: 'Thank God for those dear words! Kiss me. How I worship you for saying them!'

Hester told this incident to Hannah, who received it with a rebuking look, and said, coldly: 'Sister, it was a lie.'

Hester's lips trembled piteously; she choked down a sob, and said: 'Oh, Hannah, it was a sin, but I could not help it. I could not endure the fright and the misery that were in her face.'

'No matter. It was a lie. God will hold you to account for it.'

'Oh, I know it, I know it,' cried Hester, wringing her hands, 'but even if it were now, I could not help it. I know I should do it again.'

'Then take my place with Helen in the morning. I will make the report myself.'

Hester clung to her sister, begging and imploring.

'Don't, Hannah, oh, don't—you will kill her.'

'I will at least speak the truth.'

In the morning she had a cruel report to bear to the mother, and she braced herself for the trial. When she returned from her mission, Hester was waiting, pale and trembling, in the hall. She whispered: 'Oh, how did she take it—that poor, desolate mother?'

Hannah's eyes were swimming in tears. She said: 'God forgive me, I told her the child was well!'

Hester gathered her to her heart, with a grateful 'God bless you, Hannah!' and poured out her thankfulness in an inundation of worshiping praises. After that, the two knew the limit of their strength, and accepted their fate. They surrendered humbly, and abandoned themselves to the hard requirements of the situation. Daily they told the morning lie, and confessed their sin in prayer; not asking forgiveness, as not being worthy of it, but only wishing to make record that they realized their wickedness and were not desiring to hide it or excuse it. Daily, as the fair young idol of the house sank lower and lower, the sorrowful old aunts painted her glowing bloom and her fresh young beauty to the wan mother, and winced under the stabs her ecstasies of joy and gratitude gave them.

In the first days, while the child had strength to hold a pencil, she wrote fond little love-notes to her mother, in which she concealed her illness; and these the mother read and reread through happy eyes wet with thankful tears, and kissed them over and over again, and treasured them as precious things under her pillow. Then came a day when the strength was gone from the hand, and the mind wandered, and the tongue babbled pathetic incoherences. This was a sore dilemma for the poor aunts. There were no love-notes for the mother. They did not know what to do. Hester began a carefully studied and plausible explanation, but lost the track of it and grew confused; suspicion began to show in the mother's face, then alarm. Hester saw it, recognized the imminence of the danger, and descended to the emergency, pulling herself resolutely together and plucking victor from the open jaws of defeat. In a placid and convincing voice she said: 'I thought it might distress you to know it, but Helen spent the night at the Sloanes'. There was a little party there, and, although she did not want to go, and you so sick, we persuaded her, she being young and needing the innocent pastimes of youth, and we believing you would approve. Be sure she will write the moment she comes.'

'How good you are, and how dear and thoughtful for us both!

Approve? Why, I thank you with all my heart. My poor little exile! Tell her I want her to have every pleasure she can—I would not rob her of one. Only let her keep her health, that is all I ask. Don't let that suffer; I could not bear it. How thankful I am that she escaped this infection—and what a narrow risk she ran, Aunt Hester! Think of that lovely face all dulled and burned with fever. I can't bear the thought of it. Keep her health. Keep her bloom! I can see her now, the dainty creature—with the big, blue, earnest eyes; and sweet, oh, so sweet and gentle and winning! Is she as beautiful as ever, dear Aunt Hester?'

'Oh, more beautiful and bright and charming than ever she was before, if such a thing can be'—and Hester turned away and fumbled with the medicine-bottles, to hide her shame and grief.

CHAPTER V

After a little, both aunts were laboring upon a difficult and baffling work in Helen's chamber. Patiently and earnestly, with their stiff old fingers, they were trying to forge the required note. They made failure after failure, but they improved little by little all the time. The pity of it all, the pathetic humor of it, there was none to see; they themselves were unconscious of it. Often their tears fell upon the notes and spoiled them; sometimes a single misformed word made a note risky which could have been ventured but for that; but at last Hannah produced one whose script was a good enough imitation of Helen's to pass any but a suspicious eye, and bountifully enriched it with the petting phrases and loving nicknames that had been familiar on the child's lips from her nursery days. She carried it to the mother, who took it with avidity, and kissed it, and fondled it, reading its precious words over and over again, and dwelling with deep contentment upon its closing paragraph:

'Mousie darling, if I could only see you, and kiss your eyes, and feel your arms about me! I am so glad my practicing does not disturb you. Get well soon. Everybody is good to me, but I am so lonesome without you, dear mamma.'

'The poor child, I know just how she feels. She cannot be quite happy without me; and I—oh, I live in the light of her eyes! Tell her she must practice all she pleases; and, Aunt Hannah—tell her I can't hear the piano this far, nor hear dear voice when she sings: God knows I wish I could. No one knows how sweet that voice is to me; and to think—some day it will be silent! What are you crying for?' 'Only because—because—it was just a memory. When I came away she was singing, 'Loch Lomond.' The pathos of it! It always moves me so when she sings that.'

'And me, too. How heartbreakingly beautiful it is when some youthful sorrow is brooding in her breast and she sings it for the mystic healing it brings.... Aunt Hannah?'

'Dear Margaret?'

'I am very ill. Sometimes it comes over me that I shall never hear that dear voice again.'

'Oh, don't—don't, Margaret! I can't bear it!'

Margaret was moved and distressed, and said, gently:

'There—there—let me put my arms around you. Don't cry. There—put your cheek to mine. Be comforted. I wish to live. I will live if I can. Ah, what could she do without me!... Does she often speak of me?—but I know she does.'

'Oh, all the time—all the time!'

'My sweet child! She wrote the note the moment she came home?'

'Yes—the first moment. She would not wait to take off her things.'

'I knew it. It is her dear, impulsive, affectionate way. I knew it without asking, but I wanted to hear you say it. The petted wife knows she is loved, but she makes her husband tell her so every day, just for the joy of hearing it.... She used the pen this time. That is better; the pencil-marks could rub out, and I should grieve for that. Did you suggest that she use the pen?'

'Y—no—she—it was her own idea.'

The mother looked her pleasure, and said: 'I was hoping you would say that. There was never such a dear and thoughtful child!... Aunt Hannah?'

'Dear Margaret?'

'Go and tell her I think of her all the time, and worship her. Why—you are crying again. Don't be so worried about me, dear; I think there is nothing to fear, yet.'

The grieving messenger carried her message, and piously delivered it to unheeding ears. The girl babbled on unaware; looking up at her with wondering and startled eyes flaming with fever, eyes in which was no light of recognition: 'Are you—no, you are not my mother. I want her—oh, I want her! She was here a minute ago—I did not see her go. Will she come? Will she come quickly? Will she come now?... There are so many houses ... and they oppress me so... and everything whirls and turns and whirls... oh, my head, my head!'—and so she wandered on and on, in her pain, flitting from one torturing fancy to another, and tossing her arms about in a weary and ceaseless persecution of unrest.

Poor old Hannah wetted the parched lips and softly stroked the hot brow, murmuring endearing and pitying words, and thanking the Father of all that the mother was happy and did not know.

CHAPTER VI

Daily the child sank lower and steadily lower towards the grave, and daily the sorrowing old watchers carried gilded tidings of her radiant health and loveliness to the happy mother, whose pilgrimage was also now nearing its end. And daily they forged loving and cheery notes in the child's hand, and stood by with remorseful consciences and bleeding hearts, and wept to see the grateful mother devour them and adore them and treasure them away as things beyond price, because of their sweet source, and sacred because her child's hand had touched them.

At last came that kindly friend who brings healing and peace to all. The lights were burning low. In the solemn hush which precedes the dawn vague figures flitted soundless along the dim hall and gathered silent and awed in Helen's chamber, and grouped themselves about her bed, for a warning had gone forth, and they knew. The dying girl lay with closed lids, and unconscious, the drapery upon her breast faintly rising and falling as her wasting life ebbed away. At intervals a sigh or a muffled sob broke upon the stillness. The same haunting thought was in all minds there: the pity of this death, the going out into the great darkness, and the mother not here to help and hearten and bless.

Helen stirred; her hands began to grope wistfully about as if they sought something—she had been blind some hours. The end was come; all knew it. With a great sob Hester gathered her to her breast, crying, 'Oh, my child, my darling!' A rapturous light broke in the dying girl's face, for it was mercifully vouchsafed her to mistake those sheltering arms for another's; and she went to her rest murmuring, 'Oh, mamma, I am so happy—I longed for you—now I can die.'

Two hours later Hester made her report. The mother asked: 'How is it with the child?'

'She is well.'

CHAPTER VII

A sheaf of white crape and black was hung upon the door of the house, and there it swayed and rustled in the wind and whispered its tidings. At noon the preparation of the dead was finished, and in the coffin lay the fair young form, beautiful, and in the sweet face a great peace. Two mourners sat by it, grieving and worshipping—Hannah and the black woman Tilly. Hester came, and she was trembling, for a great trouble was upon her spirit. She said:

'She asks for a note.'

Hannah's face blanched. She had not thought of this; it had seemed that that pathetic service was ended. But she realized now that that could not be. For a little while the two women stood looking into each other's face, with vacant eyes; then Hannah said:

'There is no way out of it—she must have it; she will suspect, else.'

'And she would find out.'

'Yes. It would break her heart.' She looked at the dead face, and her eyes filled. 'I will write it,' she said.

Hester carried it. The closing line said:

'Darling Mousie, dear sweet mother, we shall soon be together again. Is not that good news? And it is true; they all say it is true.'

The mother mourned, saying:

'Poor child, how will she bear it when she knows? I shall never see her again in life. It is hard, so hard. She does not suspect? You guard her from that?'

'She thinks you will soon be well.'

'How good you are, and careful, dear Aunt Hester! None goes near her who could carry the infection?'

'It would be a crime.'

'But you SEE her?'

'With a distance between—yes.'

'That is so good. Others one could not trust; but you two guardian angels—steel is not so true as you. Others would be unfaithful; and many would deceive, and lie.'

Hester's eyes fell, and her poor old lips trembled.

'Let me kiss you for her, Aunt Hester; and when I am gone, and the danger is past, place the kiss upon her dear lips some day, and say her mother sent it, and all her mother's broken heart is in it.'

Within the hour, Hester, raining tears upon the dead face, performed her pathetic mission.

CHAPTER VIII

Another day dawned, and grew, and spread its sunshine in the earth. Aunt Hannah brought comforting news to the failing mother, and a happy note, which said again, 'We have but a little time to wait, darling mother, then we shall be together.'

The deep note of a bell came moaning down the wind.

'Aunt Hannah, it is tolling. Some poor soul is at rest. As I shall be soon. You will not let her forget me?'

'Oh, God knows she never will!'

'Do not you hear strange noises, Aunt Hannah? It sounds like the shuffling of many feet.'

'We hoped you would not hear it, dear. It is a little company gathering, for—for Helen's sake, poor little prisoner. There will be music—and she loves it so. We thought you would not mind.'

'Mind? Oh no, no—oh, give her everything her dear heart can desire. How good you two are to her, and how good to me! God bless you both always!'

After a listening pause:

'How lovely! It is her organ. Is she playing it herself, do you think?'

Faint and rich and inspiring the chords floating to her ears on the still air. 'Yes, it is her touch, dear heart, I recognize it. They are singing. Why—it is a hymn! and the sacredest of all, the most touching, the most consoling.... It seems to open the gates of paradise to me....

If I could die now....'

Faint and far the words rose out of the stillness:

Nearer, my God, to Thee,

Nearer to Thee,

E'en though it be a cross

That raiseth me.

With the closing of the hymn another soul passed to its rest, and they that had been one in life were not sundered in death. The sisters, mourning and rejoicing, said:

'How blessed it was that she never knew!'

CHAPTER IX

At midnight they sat together, grieving, and the angel of the Lord appeared in the midst transfigured with a radiance not of earth; and speaking, said: 'For liars a place is appointed. There they burn in the fires of hell from everlasting unto everlasting. Repent!'

The bereaved fell upon their knees before him and clasped their hands and bowed their gray heads, adoring. But their tongues clove to the roof of their mouths, and they were dumb.

'Speak! that I may bear the message to the chancery of heaven and bring again the decree from which there is no appeal.'

Then they bowed their heads yet lower, and one said: 'Our sin is great, and we suffer shame; but only perfect and final repentance can make us whole; and we are poor creatures who have learned our human weakness, and we know that if we were in those hard straits again our hearts would fail again, and we should sin as before. The strong could prevail, and so be saved, but we are lost.'

They lifted their heads in supplication. The angel was gone. While they marveled and wept he came again; and bending low, he whispered the decree.

CHAPTER X

Was it Heaven? Or Hell?

ABOUT TERRY O'BRIEN

Terry O'Brien is an academic with three decades of experience in teaching language and communication skills in India and abroad. He also headed a college under the auspices of the University of Delhi.

A prolific writer, with several books to his credit, Terry O'Brien is a reputed professional motivational speaker and a quizmaster.